SPEECHLESS

Also by Valerie Sherrard:

The Shelby Belgarden Mystery Series:
Out of the Ashes
In Too Deep
Chasing Shadows
Hiding in Plain Sight
Eyes of a Stalker

Other Books:
Kate
Sam's Light
Sarah's Legacy

Forthcoming:
Three Million Acres of Flame (Fall, 2007)

SPEECHLESS

by Valerie Sherrard

A BOARDWALK BOOK
A MEMBER OF THE DUNDURN GROUP
TORONTO

Editor: Barry Jowett
Designer: Erin Mallory
Proofreader: Marja Appleford
Cover Illustration: David Jardine
Printer: Webcom

Library and Archives Canada Cataloguing in Publication

Sherrard, Valerie
    Speechless / Valerie Sherrard.
ISBN 978-1-55002-701-3
    1. Public speaking--Juvenile fiction. I. Title.

PS8587.H3867S64 2007   jC813'.6   C2007-900861-5

2   3   4   5   11   10   09   08

 Conseil des Arts du Canada   Canada Council for the Arts   Canada    ONTARIO ARTS COUNCIL CONSEIL DES ARTS DE L'ONTARIO

We acknowledge the support of the **Canada Council for the Arts** and the **Ontario Arts Council** for our publishing program. We also acknowledge the financial support of the **Government of Canada** through the **Book Publishing Industry Development Program** and **The Association for the Export of Canadian Books**, and the **Government of Ontario** through the **Ontario Book Publishers Tax Credit program** and the **Ontario Media Development Corporation**.

Printed and bound in Canada
www.dundurn.com

Dundurn Press	Gazelle Book Services Limited	Dundurn Press
3 Church Street, Suite 500	White Cross Mills	2250 Military Road
Toronto, Ontario, Canada	High Town, Lancaster, England	Tonawanda, NY
M5E 1M2	LA1 4XS	U.S.A. 14150

*This book is dedicated with love
to my very talented son-in-law,
David Jardine,
who illustrated the cover.*

CHAPTER ONE

If you asked my parents or friends or even one of my sisters to describe me they'd most likely sum me up in one word:

Quiet.

I guess I am.

Fact is, I don't like to draw attention to myself. And, as a person whose main goal is to make sure people don't notice me, it pretty much follows that I don't talk a whole lot. No one pays much attention to you if you don't have much to say, so there was no way I could have predicted what would happen when I stopped talking *altogether*.

The whole thing started because of an English assignment we got back in January, when Mr. Furlong announced that it was time for us to start working on our oratory presentations.

I broke out in a sweat right there at my desk, second from the back, third row from the door. It was a bit early to be panicking, so the cold chill that ran through me seemed like a bad sign. The first part of the assignment — which was writing the speech — wasn't due for a week, and we wouldn't start delivering them in front of the class for another week or so after that. Even so, I found my hands getting clammy and hot prickles creeping along my neck.

You'd understand *why* if you'd been here to see what happened last year.

It was our first time doing speeches and when our English teacher, Miss Harlan, gave us the assignment it didn't even seem like such a big deal. We only had to come up with a two-minute talk and it could be on anything we wanted. I wasn't thrilled, but I sure didn't picture it turning out the way it did.

The first mistake I made was mentioning it at home when we were eating dinner that night. Actually, all I did was ask my sister, Kellie, who's one grade ahead of me, if her class had done speeches the year before.

"Don't you *remember*, you moron?" she said, rolling her eyes. I shouldn't have expected anything else.

"In this family, we do *not* call each other names," Mom said, though, obviously, that wasn't true. Then she turned to me and said, "She did her speech on Kalan Porter. You must remember her practising it."

"It probably didn't, you know, stand out in his mind, since that's all she *ever* talks about," said my oldest sister, Nicole. She rolled her eyes and gave a huge sigh to show

how tiresome this was to her. Nicole is in grade eleven. Everything bores her.

"Kellie *loves* Kalan," chimed in Leah, my third and final sister, and the baby of the family. She's not quite four and goes to pre-kindergarten, though we have to call it "school" in front of her or she goes mental.

"Why? Is your class doing speeches?" Kellie asked.

"Yeah," I mumbled. I wished I hadn't brought it up.

"Griffin is going to give a speech," Mom said to Dad.

"Hungh," said Dad, who was sitting right there and had heard the whole thing.

"He will make *such* a fool of himself," Kellie predicted.

"Now, Kellie, that's no way to talk." Mom gave her a warning look. "Griffin will do just fine, won't you, dear? What are you going to do your speech on?"

I shrugged and ate faster.

"You know," Mom said, "I used to get really good marks in English when I was in school."

Like I hadn't heard that before — maybe a couple of thousand times.

"I *enjoy* writing, and I'm really, well, quite good at it." She smiled and tried to look modest. "Why don't I help you with your speech?"

"Uh, that's okay," I said.

"It's no trouble, really. In fact, I'd *love* to do it." She smiled at me. "It will be *nice* for us to do something together, don't you think?"

There's no right answer to a question like that. I

shrugged and said, "I guess." Even Mom should have been able to see that my enthusiasm was at a record low.

"Wonderful!" Mom said. "Why don't we get started as soon as the dishes are done?"

Something you should know about my mom: when she gets an idea in her head, there's no shaking it. Or her. After a couple of hours, during which she made suggestions and forced me to listen to sample paragraphs on a bunch of different subjects, I did something even stupider than mentioning it in the first place: I gave in. Or, as my best friend Bryan said when I told him about it later, I capitulated.

In my defence, by that time I hardly knew *what* I was doing. I just wanted the torture to end. But when the confusion lifted from my brain I discovered that the topic I'd agreed to was *not*, as I'd thought, interplanetary travel. Instead, it was some stupid thing about men being from Mars and women being from Venus.

I still didn't know what that meant until Mom brought out this book with a dorky-looking guy on the cover and started writing stuff down. She was on her third paragraph when I realized the book was about *relationships*!

"Hey!" I said. "*This* isn't about space travel."

"Of course it isn't, dear," Mom said, barely glancing at me.

"Well, I don't wanna talk about this ... this ... *stuff!*"

"You see!" Mom said like she'd just proven a point. "That's *exactly* what we're talking about here."

I protested and complained and I swear I wasn't one bit swayed when she told me that the girls would think I was cool because of it. Okay, I might have been influenced a *little bit* when she mentioned April Saunders, who sat in front of me in class last year.

I probably don't need to tell you that when speech day came and it was my turn to get up in front of the class I found myself mumbling that the topic I had "chosen" to speak on was the difference between how men and women communicate.

The snickering started almost immediately. By the time I'd made my miserable way through to the third prompt card everyone was laughing. That was when I dropped the cue cards. I bent over, scooped them from the floor, and kept reading. Somehow my brain failed to kick up the message that the cards were now in random order.

When I finally realized I was repeating myself, I stopped in the middle of a sentence and flipped to the next one. When I heard myself rereading the opening line I stopped, tried to reorganize them, and somehow managed to end up reading it a third time. The class howled. Even Miss Harlan was struggling to keep from laughing.

It went downhill after that.

I pressed on, knowing that I'd have to repeat the whole experience if I didn't. I read unconnected things from out-of-order cards until the timekeeper mercifully signalled that my time was up. As I stumbled back toward my seat, it felt less like I was moving down the aisle, and more like the entire room was rushing toward me.

Thinking back on that whole fiasco, it's no wonder the thought of another performance in front of the class was enough to send me into a spin. By the time the bell rang to dismiss us that day, my mind was made up.

I *had* to find a way out of it.

CHAPTER TWO

I spent the next two days thinking through possibilities, but every idea I came up with had serious flaws. For example, I thought of trying to fool everyone into thinking I had laryngitis. You can't give a speech if you can't talk.

Problem with that was that Mom would drag me off to Doctor Stephens and I could just picture a whole bunch of tests being done. Swabs and x-rays and blood work and who knows what else. I'd get caught for sure, and I didn't even want to *think* about what would happen then.

It was Bryan who came up with the variation on the lost-voice idea, and I recognized right away that it was brilliant.

"What," he said, "if you couldn't talk for some *other* reason, something people wouldn't be able to challenge?"

"But not a sore throat?"

"Nah," he said, a grin growing on his face. "A cause."

"Huh?"

"A *cause*, dude. You need to go on a protest. Of silence."

"You mean some kind of religious thing?" I was doubtful, but interested.

"Nuh-uh, not religious," he paused. "Social. A social cause of some sort."

"Like what?"

"Let's see what's popular these days." He stood, took a couple of steps across the room and plunked down at his computer.

"There's lots of stuff to choose from," he said as he typed in key words on Metacrawler, his favourite search engine. "We've got women's rights, endangered species, ethnic groups, children's rights, all kinds of social issues. You name it, I can find you an issue. The tough part will be narrowing it down. You got any ideas?"

"Not women's rights," I said quickly, flashing back to the Mars and Venus thing. I knew it wasn't the same, but it just seemed best to steer clear of another subject that had anything to do with women.

He thought for a few seconds and then typed in "human rights" and tapped enter. I might as well mention that Bryan is like some kind of genius or something. He can read a page in the time it takes me to get through a paragraph, and he never seems to forget anything. I just sat back and waited for him to finish what he was doing. No sense in two of us wasting all that energy and brainpower.

He browsed through a few links and then straightened up a bit when he'd entered one about halfway down the page. Clicking on the story he leaned forward and scanned the article.

"I think we've got it," he said. "Here, in the Amnesty International site, there's a story about kids in the army."

"Yeah?"

"Little kids being forced to fight in wars. In African countries."

"Oh, yeah?" I'd thought Africa *was* a country, but I didn't say that to him.

"Uh huh. There's a bunch of 'em." Bryan looked pleased as he printed a couple of pages out and passed them to me. "That oughta do it. I mean, we don't want to waste too much time on your bogus reason for not talking. This looks good enough to me."

I read the few paragraphs he'd given me and had to agree. Still, there was a problem.

"How am I going to explain how I heard about it in the first place?"

"Browsing, man," Bryan said. "Just stay vague. Act like you read about it and, I dunno, it got to you or something. So you decided to take a stand."

I liked the sound of that. Taking a stand. It seemed brave and strong.

So it was settled. I'd take this vow of silence and stop

talking altogether until the oratory thing was over and done. Mr. Furlong could hardly expect me to break a *vow* just for a stupid assignment, could he?

"Okay, you've got two choices on how to let people know what you're doing," Bryan went on. "You can tell your folks and ask them to pass the word along to the school, or you can write something up and just let people read it."

I knew, of course, that when he said I could write something up, he meant *he'd* do it. I went with that option and he turned back to the computer, typing, reading, editing, and working away at it until it seemed he was satisfied.

"I'll save it on my drive in case you need another copy," he said after he'd printed out a copy for me to sign and use. "Read it first, though, in case you want something changed."

I glanced through it, amazed (even though I'd seen stuff like this from Bryan before) at the amount of detail he remembered from glancing through the information he'd found earlier. He hadn't even gone back to double check anything but I knew what he had there was dead on.

What he'd written was great. Too great.

"I think you put too much in here," I said. "It makes it sound like I know a lot about this, and I don't. What if people ask me questions about it?"

"You mean when you're not talking and can't answer

them anyway?" Bryan asked, smirking.

"Oh, yeah." I thought for a minute. "Still, it's going to look suspicious. No one's going to believe I wrote this. It's too good."

"I guess you're right," he said. "So, what do you think — I should dumb it down to make it more convincing?"

I nodded. "Just make it short and to the point, like I heard about this and I'm protesting it, period."

He went back to work, chopping and rewriting. When he hit the print command again the page that zipped out had only about a fifth of the original message. It was also written in a much simpler style than his first attempt.

Here's what it said:

PROTEST OF SILENCE!

Should *kids* be fighting in wars? *No way*!!! But they are!!! Believe it or not, this is happening right now in a number of African countries. And it's time for someone to take a stand! So that's what I'm doing! I, Griffin John Maxwell, will not speak again until something has been done about this.

Beneath that were places for me to add my signature and the date. I looked it over again, signed and dated it, folded the page, and stuck it into my back pocket.

"The italics and exclamation marks really make it sound like you're outraged," Bryan said. "Don't you think?"

"Yeah, it's great. Thanks. I guess I might as well head home and see how it goes over there."

"No prob. Good luck, dude."

I said thanks again but I didn't really think I'd need much luck. After all, what could go wrong?

CHAPTER THREE

I weighed the pros and cons of waiting until bedtime before giving my "protest" sheet to Mom, just in case I felt like saying something before then. Then I realized they'd wonder why I'd been talking at all if I'd had this thing done up earlier. I mean, if I had really taken a vow of silence, it would have started as soon as I'd made up my mind. So, I gave Mom the paper and stood there while she read it.

"Protest of Silence," she read out loud. Then her lips moved without sound as she read the rest. When she was finished she turned to me.

"Well, my goodness, Griffin! I had no idea that you even knew anything about social issues, much less felt this strongly about them."

I almost answered, and just clamped my mouth shut at the last second. Instead, I tried to look serious and concerned, and nodded.

"Well, isn't that nice, dear," she said. She patted

my head, something she *knows* I hate. "I must go tell your father."

She disappeared down the hall with my paper flapping in her hand.

I hadn't expected much in the way of a reaction from Dad. He mostly tries to avoid things as much as he can around here. I think it's because every time Mom drags him into the middle of something, it turns on him somehow. Especially if it's anything to do with us kids.

But he came along down the hall, and stopped in front of me. He was holding my paper and he kind of squatted down in front of me and looked me straight in the eye.

"This is really something, Griffin," he said. Then he shook my hand.

I felt proud for a few seconds. Then I remembered that the protest wasn't real and I mostly felt like a big jerk.

But I reminded myself that it didn't matter, really. It would all be over in a matter of weeks and everything would go back to normal. No harm done.

Dad gave me back my paper and stood there for a few more seconds before returning to whatever it is that he does in the back room. It used to be a playroom for us kids but now there's a rec room downstairs — mostly full of Leah's stuff, of course. The rest of us just hang out there with friends sometimes.

Dad took over the room out back, moving in a desk and a couple of old wing chairs, some bookcases, and Nicole's old CD player. Mom says no one wants to hear his music anyway and that it's just as well he keeps it to himself. I've heard some of it and I have to agree with Mom on this one.

Things had gone a lot easier than I'd expected with my folks. Not that I thought they were going to freak or anything, but I *had* expected them to ask some questions. Instead, while they'd seemed kind of happy about it, it felt like they'd really under-reacted.

When I found out why that was, it kind of made me mad. That happened the next day. It was a Saturday and I'd woken up earlier than usual for a weekend morning. I lay there for a while — kind of waiting — but when I saw that I wasn't going to be able to fall back to sleep, I headed down the hall toward the bathroom.

Mom and Dad were in the kitchen, talking. Normally, I'd never pay attention to that, but I heard my name so I stopped and listened.

"You don't suppose it will last until Monday, do you?" Mom said.

"Hard to say," Dad said. I could picture him there with the newspaper, trying to read and talk to Mom at the same time, like he does most mornings.

"I wouldn't be surprised if he's forgotten all about it by this morning," Mom went on. "I mean, it was a really nice thought, but I can't see him sticking to it."

"Probably not." I heard the paper rustle.

"He doesn't even have a plan of action."

"So I noticed."

"If he was really serious, he'd have thought that through, don't you think?"

"Probably." The paper snapped, the way it does when Dad flicks open a new section.

"I wanted to ask him that yesterday, but it was such a thoughtful idea, it would have been a shame to put a damper on it." Mom tapped her spoon on the rim of a cup. "But if he *does* happen to persist with this, he'll have to come up with something concrete."

"Well, of course," Dad agreed. "He can't just stop talking without something specific to work toward."

"We'll just see what happens. If it turns out to be a problem we'll deal with it then, but I don't think we have much to worry about."

"He's a good kid, that Griffin," my dad said then, though how that was related to what Mom was saying I have no idea. "Not like some of the young lads these days."

"Yes, imagine him even *thinking* of doing something like this. He must have been genuinely touched by the plight of those children."

By then I'd heard enough. I crept back to my room and stretched out on the covers, arms folded over my head.

My stomach was churning but I can't always tell if that means I'm mad or embarrassed or what. It really bugged me that it was so easy for them to think I'd take a vow of silence one day and then forget all about it the next. Didn't say much for their faith in me.

Of course, it was hard to stay indignant about that when my brain kept reminding me that the whole thing was a lie. It's funny how ashamed you can feel even when nobody else is there, judging you. I could see that it would be easy to get bogged down in the guilt, and end up blowing the whole thing.

Only, I couldn't let that happen.

I turned it all around in my head for a bit until I'd persuaded myself that it was no big deal and I couldn't be letting it get to me. I'd get out of making the speech, and that was the only thing that *really* mattered. Still, it was a bit disappointing to know my parents didn't believe I could actually do it.

When I got up later on everyone was in the kitchen except for Kellie who had slept over at her best friend Ariel's place. I never could understand how the two of them got to be friends, since they're totally opposite. Ariel is cool and fun and really hot. Kellie is none of those things. On the hot scale she's actually in the negative.

Not that I mind that they hang out together. It means Ariel is around sometimes, and she always talks to me normal, not like stupid old Kellie who acts as though being fourteen months older than a person makes her superior in every way.

That wasn't my worry this morning, though, as I grabbed a bowl from the cupboard and plunked into a chair at the table. I waited for someone to say "good morning" so I could have a chance to *not* answer, but no one did.

"Griffin is a big lazy bum," Leah announced point-lessly. She jabbed her spoon in my general direction as she spoke, slopping milk and Cheerios off it. That took her attention from me. She said "OH-OH!" and grabbed a couple of napkins to wipe up the mess.

I poured myself some cereal and pretended I didn't notice Mom and Dad exchanging a glance and then trying to act like they weren't watching to see what I was going to do. I started eating.

"What's wrong with *you*?"

I glanced up to see Nicole staring at me. It surprised me because I hadn't done anything — not really — and yet she'd somehow picked up that something was different.

I shook my head while I chewed. Nicole frowned. She was about to say something else when Mom cut in.

"Griffin has taken a vow of silence," Mom told her. "For child soldiers in Africa."

I barely managed to stop myself from correcting her by saying, "It's a *protest*, Mom."

"He is *so* weird," Nicole said. "He's not doing it out-side the house though, right? I mean, you're not letting him carry on like this at *school*."

"Well, I, uh ...," Mom glanced at me like I might speak up and answer for her.

"You don't even go to the same school," Dad pointed out.

"No, they're only right next to each other, and anyway, word gets around. I will be *so* humiliated if people hear about my brother doing something this ridiculous!" Nicole stood up and came over to my side, standing practically on top of me and leaning down. Her face was almost touching mine.

"You pull this stunt at school and you will be *so* sorry," she said. Then she stomped out of the room.

Her threat hung there, making my stomach kind of squeeze tight. It was just as well that I didn't know an irate sister would be the least of my worries at school.

CHAPTER FOUR

The trouble started before I'd even made it to class on Monday morning. I was at my locker, twirling the dial back to eleven when Bo Werner came by.

"Hey, Griff," he says. "You got your Math done?"

I'm sure I don't have to tell you that Bo wasn't asking this because he was all concerned about the state of my grades or anything. He wanted to copy my answers so he wouldn't get a detention for not having his homework done. Again.

It would have been okay if I'd had my Math notebook with me. In that case, I'd just have handed it over (like always) and that would have been the end of it. I mean, Bo wasn't looking for conversation — the notebook, passed over without a word, would have satisfied him.

Unfortunately, I didn't have the work with me. I'd finished the questions on Friday and passed the book in to Mr. Durkin. But of course, I couldn't tell that to Bo without talking.

Instead, I shook my head sideways and held up both hands, palms out, to show him that I didn't have the book.

"What do you mean, 'NO'?" he said, making it sound like I'd yelled the word out, which I obviously had not done.

I made a few more gestures, shrugged, waved my hands around, and did my best to get the message across. I even raised my eyebrows a few times, though it wasn't clear, even to me, what that was supposed to mean. Bo just stood there staring and looking madder and madder.

"Don't think you're getting away with this," he muttered. Then he walked away. I was surprised he hadn't hauled off and ploughed me one right then and there until I saw Mademoiselle Gallipeau, one of the French teachers, in the hallway behind me.

I headed to class trying to convince myself that once he heard about my protest of silence he'd realize I hadn't been blowing him off. It didn't make me feel any better though, and the hot/cold lump that was growing in my gut told me it wasn't going to be that simple. Bo isn't the most reasonable guy at Westingford Middle School.

My first encounter with Bo went way back to second grade, when he swiped the caramel cakes Mom had put in my lunch. I didn't know the way things worked back then, so I marched right up to him and demanded them back. His response was to shove one of the cakes into his mouth whole and laugh while bits of chocolate and cake burst into the air around him. At the same time, he swatted the top of my head the way you might whack a fly that's annoying you.

That was about as close as Bo ever came to negotiating. He got what he wanted. You either gave it to him willingly or he took it and laughed in your face.

I got to class and slid into my seat, still thinking about how I was going to get things cleared up with Bo without any bloodshed (mine), which actually made me almost forget about the whole not-speaking deal. It hardly registered when Mr. Simons started talking.

"Class!" he said, tapping his ruler on the desk to get our attention. "Before we begin today's History lesson, I have a little announcement."

Then, to my horror, he launched into a big explanation of how I was taking a stand, trying to make a difference in the world by making a personal sacrifice.

"Giving up the right of speech," he went on, "is no small thing. Speech, as our primary means of communication, is one of the fundamental freedoms in the free world. Why, the very voice of democracy depends on one's ability to engage in free speech."

I willed him to stop.

"And yet, young Griffin has chosen to set aside this right, to protest injustice in countries where the freedoms we enjoy do not exist," he continued. "In taking this vow of silence, he has risen his voice high."

Everyone was staring by then. I wished I could shrink out of sight. Then he wrapped it up by insisting that everyone clap for me. And of course, they did. They had no choice.

After that it was just about impossible to hear anything Simons said as he raved away about the Loyalists. All through class I could feel the eyes on me — curious glances and outright stares.

Lunch hour was a nightmare. At least half a dozen kids came up to me in the first five minutes and asked me why I'd quit talking. They actually seemed surprised and kind of put out when I didn't answer them! Real sharp, huh?

Mira Travis made a big deal of coming over and telling me how much she admired what I was doing, like I didn't know she was just saying that because she likes me — a feeling that is definitely *not* mutual. She sends one of her geeky friends to tell me that "someone likes me but they can't say who" about once a week. I always tell them I couldn't care less, which, for some reason, makes them giggle. Then they go directly back to Mira where they put their heads close together and whisper while they peek at me and giggle some more.

"I mean, it's *really* cool," she said. She smiled and did something weird with her eyes and then looked down like she was all shy or something. I'm sure you can understand why I might not exactly buy the shy act.

Bryan has a few names for her friends.

"Alert! Here comes one of Mira's Minions," he'll say, with no effort to hide his smirk. It's easy for him to find it funny, since he's not the one being tortured. "Don't they kind of remind you of the winged monkeys in *The Wizard of Oz?*"

At the moment, though, Bryan was nowhere in sight and Mira was leaning in with her creepy smile. It seemed that she was waiting for some kind of response from me, even though she knew I couldn't say anything.

I shifted uncomfortably and glanced around. That was when I saw Bryan, half hidden behind one of the pillars that stand along the open side of the cafeteria. He realized I'd spotted him and came out, sauntering over like he hadn't just been having a laugh at my expense.

"I've gotta talk to Griff about something," he said to Mira as he slid into a seat at the table. "Sorry."

She looked miffed but she left. I figured that was what mattered anyway. Of course, that was before Bryan explained he'd been skulking about not, as I'd assumed, to enjoy watching me squirm, but because he'd overheard something important.

"Seems that Bo Werner is out to get you," he told me. "I heard Glen Massey taking bets on how long it takes you to hit the ground."

CHAPTER FIVE

I opened my mouth to say something but snapped it shut when I remembered I couldn't talk. Somehow, with everything else going on, I'd managed to forget that Bo was mad at me.

Since I couldn't speak, I just sat there and tried *not* to think about what Bo might be planning. Like that was possible. My mind kept drifting back to the last fight I'd seen him in. From what I could remember, Bo wasn't a big fan of fighting clean and fair.

It also didn't help that he was twice my size.

Not that Bo has ever in his whole life fought someone who was anywhere near as big as him. He likes 'em scrawny and scared, and I hate to brag, but I fill that order quite nicely.

For a few seconds, I told myself that this could still be worked out — that Bo could be reasoned with. But I knew better.

A sudden memory came to me of the summer before and a scene at the wharf when Bo decided he'd like to fly Avery Lafferty's remote plane. Avery had just gotten it for his birthday and Avery's family is kind of poor, so the plane was a pretty big deal to him.

Now, growing up around here most of us knew how things worked, but Avery had never had anything Bo wanted before, so he wasn't used to the rules. If he'd known, he'd have handed over the plane and hoped it came back in one piece. I'd have given the plane a fifty-fifty chance if that had happened.

Only Avery didn't hand over the plane. And that was a bad move. Bo shoved him around and got the plane anyway (like everyone except Avery knew he would) and he flew it for a while and when he got bored, he smashed it to smithereens (once again, like everyone else knew he would). Then he shoved Avery to the ground and laughed in his face.

As you can see, Bo doesn't care to be told "no." And that's exactly what he thought I'd just told him.

If I'd been able to explain the whole thing to Bryan, he might have come up with a solution. I'm sure you've already noticed that he's more of an idea guy than I am.

Since I couldn't talk, I just sat there and tried to swallow the sandwich Mom had packed in my lunch. It was leftover meatloaf and mustard, a favourite of mine, but I have to say that this one was kind of dry and tasteless. Maybe Mom left something out.

"So, how'd you manage to put Bo in the mood to pulverize you?" Bryan asked.

I pointed to my mouth and made a face to remind him that I couldn't answer. He smacked himself on the forehead with an open palm and then leaned toward me.

"Stop at my place after school," he hissed. "You can tell me everything then."

And I'd *just* reminded him that I couldn't talk. To send a stronger message, I scrunched my eyebrows together and tilted my head at a forty-five degree angle. Kind of a "Frown of Confusion." Try it for yourself; you'll see how obvious it looks. But not, apparently, to Bryan.

"What's the matter with *you*?" Bryan asked.

I added a shrug. Surely he'd get that! He leaned back a bit, like I had something contagious. I sighed and went back to the earlier signal of pointing to my mouth.

"You can talk around *me*," he whispered, rolling his eyes. "I know what's going on, remember?"

I nodded, feeling a bit foolish. He was right. There was no reason I couldn't talk if it was just me and Bryan. Still, the idea of talking made me a little uneasy, almost as if the protest of silence was real. On the other hand, I could definitely use some help. This whole thing was getting complicated.

The afternoon dragged by with me trying to concentrate on what the teachers were saying instead of thinking about how I was about to get my head pounded in. You can probably guess how easy that was.

One thing I hadn't been able to find out was exactly *when* Bo was going to whale on me, so when school let out I went out the back exit, through some hedges, and out onto Beemont Street instead of taking my usual route along King. If Bo was planning an after-school attack, that would probably be enough to throw him off for a couple of days. Eventually, though, even he would figure out the alternative-route thing and send some of his friends to guard the other doors.

I skulked along, keeping a close eye out, just in case, and made my way to Bryan's place. There was no answer when I rang the bell, so I sat on the step and waited.

It was a good ten minutes before he showed up. "Hey, I waited for you!" he said when he saw me. "How'd you get here?"

When I didn't answer he nodded knowingly and unlocked the door to let us into the house. Once inside he turned to me expectantly and said, "So, what's going on?"

Before I could answer, we heard a car door slam and a minute later Bryan's mom came breezing through the front door, her arms full of bags and parcels. As soon as she spied us her face lit right up. I don't think it was because she was all that happy to see *us* exactly. More like she was glad that there was someone around to help with the bags.

We carried them to the kitchen and were about to take off to Bryan's room where we could talk without her hearing when she made it clear we weren't finished.

"It *sure* would be nice to have help getting all of this put away," she said. In that tone mothers use. "That way I can get dinner started."

Bryan gave me a look that said there was no way around it, which I understood perfectly. It's not like I don't have a mother, too.

We'd just finished and were about to make our escape when we were given yet another task.

"Oh, boys, I know you won't mind waiting here while I make a quick call in the next room. I just need someone to stir this pasta every couple of minutes so it won't stick together. And see that the pot doesn't boil over. I'll just be a minute."

Bryan glanced at his watch and shook his head. "You have to be home at the normal time?"

I nodded. It was too risky to talk with his mother just a room away.

"Well, then, we've got about ten minutes, tops. You'd better write out what you wanted to tell me," he whispered. "My mom is *never* fast on the phone."

I hauled a sheet of paper out of my binder and started scribbling out the details of what had happened with Bo and the Math homework.

"I might be able to take care of this," Bryan said once he'd read it. "I'll explain it all to Bo and, uh, well obviously you'd have to offer him something. Otherwise, you *know* he can't just forget it after telling everyone he was going to beat you up."

He was right, but I couldn't help thinking that the way he'd said it made it sound like Bo was being totally reasonable.

"Hey, I know. You can offer to do his Math for him for a week." He frowned. "No, that won't be long enough. How about two weeks?"

I shook my head wildly.

"You think *longer*?" Bryan said, misunderstanding. "A month, then?"

I nearly busted a gasket motioning to let him know that wasn't even close to what I'd meant. That made him laugh. I saw that he'd just been messing with me. I was *not* amused.

"Take it easy, Griff," he said, "I'm just joking. But seriously, you're going to have to do something for him or he *will* pound on you."

I had no doubt about that. There was no way Bo was going to back down unless he could go around bragging about what I was doing for him in order to save my neck.

In the end, we worked it out that Bryan would make him the offer of a week of Math and see what happened. Before I left for home I *reluctantly* agreed to double that if it was absolutely necessary.

CHAPTER SIX

I couldn't help but think how weird it was — the way it worked out that I didn't get a chance to talk to Bryan. This might sound crazy, but it was almost as if some outside force had made me keep my protest of silence.

I was thinking about that when I heard my name being called. For a second, I thought it was Bo but when I turned to look it was only Reggie Bertrand barrelling down the street.

It wasn't the threatening sight I'd expected to see, but it still made me uneasy because Reggie isn't the most co-ordinated guy around. Seeing him hurtling toward me like some out-of-control meteorite didn't exactly calm my jumping nerves. I dodged.

"GRIFFIN!" he shouted when he'd lurched to a stop. I noticed that it was *exactly* where I'd been standing a second ago.

"AM I EVER GLAD TO SEE YOU!" He was gasping, half bent over from the exertion. I figured that was the fastest he'd moved since Suzanne Breau put a grass snake down his shirt in grade four.

I stood still and waited for him catch his breath, mainly because there wasn't much else I *could* do. If I started to walk away he'd only follow, trying to get out whatever he wanted to say — one loudly gasped word at a time. (Bryan calls Reggie "The Amplifier" because he yells *everything*. Even his whispers are noisy.)

"OH, MAN!" he said at last, "DID YOU KNOW THAT BO WERNER IS AFTER YOU?"

I nodded, disgusted that I'd stood there and waited, only to find out *that* was the big news flash. I should have known. If Reggie has heard something, there probably aren't many people left who haven't.

"SO, ANYWAY, I WAS THINKING, YOU COULD GET HURT!"

Brilliant.

"BEST WAY *NOT* TO GET HURT WOULD BE TO TAKE A DIVE. FIRST PUNCH, YOU SHOULD GO DOWN." He broke into a wide, sloppy smile at that, proud to have offered me this great advice.

I shrugged and started to walk away, but Reggie staggered along beside me and kept up his campaign.

"YOU THINK YOU MIGHT DO THAT THEN? HUH, GRIFFIN? THINK YOU MIGHT TAKE A DIVE FIRST PUNCH?"

Something wasn't right.

It made sense that Reggie would want to tell me Bo

was out to get me — just in case I hadn't already heard it. But it made no sense that he'd be trying to make sure I didn't get hurt too badly. It's not like we were friends or anything. It only took me a few more seconds to figure out what was going on. It was almost guaranteed that Reggie had bet on me going down after the first punch — and now he was putting on a big show like he didn't want me to get hurt when all he really wanted to do was win the pot.

I looked him right in the eye and nodded as if I was thankful for the advice. His big round face lit up and he stuck his hand out like we'd made some kind of brotherhood pact. I forced myself to shake his clammy hand before making a signal that I had to get going.

"DON'T FORGET," he roared as I walked away, "FIRST PUNCH!"

It was a good thing I couldn't talk, because I might not have been able to control myself from saying some of the things that were going through my head right about then.

I knew one thing: If Bo did decide to go ahead and pound on me, there was no way I was going down after one punch. Supposing he hit me right off with a hay-maker and knocked me out cold, I'd somehow force myself to stay upright, unconscious or not, until he'd hit me again.

Reggie Bertrand wasn't going to finance his next pizza binge courtesy of Griffin Maxwell. Besides, I could take a beating if I had to, but *no way* was I going to be branded a coward.

Mom had already dished up the food when I got home and I slid into my place just in time for Leah to recite, "God is great, God is good, Let us thank Him for the food." That's our everyday grace. When we have company, Mom always asks Dad to bless the food, and then he says, "Lord, for what we are about to receive, make us truly thankful." We all say "Amen" at the end either way. Then we dig in.

On this particular day we *did* have company but it wasn't the kind that counted for Dad to say grace. Kellie's friend, Ariel, was seated next to her — and directly across from me. She smiled and gave me a little wave with her hand.

"I guess you can't say hello," she said.

I shook my head and put a regretful look on my face to let her know I really would have liked to speak to her.

"*Look* at the reject's face!" Kellie said. She turned to Mom. "*Now* can you see what a weirdo he is! Can't you *do* something with him?"

"Now, dear. That's no way to talk about your brother," Mom said. She smiled at me, like we were humouring Kellie together.

"Sorry my brother is such a moron," Kellie said to Ariel.

"I think what he's doing is nice." Ariel smiled at me. Again!

40

"Tell Griffin *I* think it's nice too," Leah said, raising her voice.

"Just because the doofus isn't talking doesn't mean he can't *hear* you," Kellie said, rolling her eyes. "Honestly!"

She looked like she couldn't take much more and I got a happy picture in my head of her tied up in a straight jacket, being dragged out screaming.

"There's no need for that kind of talk," Mom said. "Anyway, how did your day go at school, Griffin?"

"NAH! HA! HA! You forgot!" Leah said, banging the table with the palm of her hand. "He can't talk ... 'member?"

"Oh, yes. My goodness," Mom laughed merrily to show us all what a good sport she was. "Well, but we do need to communicate somehow, now don't we? Let me think ..."

It was impossible to imagine what kind of insane idea she might come up with, but one thing was guaranteed: it would be something humiliating. I tried to eat quickly so I could escape from the table.

"I know! How about if we ask questions that only have 'yes' or 'no' answers, and you can clap! Clap once for 'yes' and twice for 'no.'"

"This is ridiculous," Nicole said. "He's not a trained seal, Mom!"

"No. Seals are a lot smarter," Kellie offered.

Surely, I thought, somebody will mention that Mom's code idea is stupid, considering that all I'd have to do is nod or shake my head for "yes" and "no." But no. Instead of anyone offering a normal, sensible solution like that, it got worse.

"I know, I know! He can *bark* if he means 'yes' and *meow* if he means 'no,'" Leah suggested. She tilted her head sideways and smiled like she was waiting for someone to tell her what a great idea that was. I kicked at her under the table.

"Ouch!"

Instead of Leah, I'd hit Ariel. Startled by the attack, she looked across the table questioningly. If she'd had any doubt as to who had kicked her, I think I dispelled it by turning red and keeping my eyes glued to my plate until I'd finished forcing down my food.

The second the last bite was shovelled in I pushed my chair back and bolted from the room. Behind me I heard Kellie saying that *honestly*, she doesn't even feel like she can bring friends over anymore and why can't we just be normal.

I stayed out of sight until I knew Ariel was gone but when I ventured back out of my room there was another problem facing me. Mom and Dad cornered me and wanted to know exactly what I was planning — besides not talking.

"You have to have some kind of game plan," Mom said.

"Your protest says you're maintaining your silence until 'something' is done," Dad pointed out. "But it's not enough for you to just quit talking. You've got to be working toward that 'something' yourself. So, we just need to know what it is."

I managed to put them off by writing a note saying that I was working on it — as if I was spending a lot of time thinking up a plan. That seemed to satisfy them for the moment, but I doubted I could hold them off for a few weeks without coming up with more than that.

I had some trouble getting to sleep that night. There were so many little problems to think about. Mostly, I couldn't get rid of the thought that, as far as this whole non-talking thing went, it hadn't exactly gotten off to the best start.

CHAPTER SEVEN

I figured that Bo would be somewhere nearby, lurking — watching for me — the next morning on my way to school. I decided he'd expect me to come late, trying to avoid him by getting to school after everyone had gone to class. It was just a guess, but trying to stay one step ahead of him was all I could do until Bryan had a chance to talk to him.

So, instead of going late, I got there a good half hour before the first bell. There were only a few kids around and there was no sign of Bo or his goons. I stayed in the boy's bathroom until I knew Bryan would have arrived and then I joined him out in the schoolyard.

"Any sign of the Neanderthal?" he asked. I shook my head, fighting a quick rush of disappointment, even though I'd known it was unlikely Bryan would have had a chance to find and talk to Bo before then.

"Yeah, well, don't worry. You know how lazy he is. He'll probably go for the homework offer."

I tried to look optimistic, but I wasn't as confident as Bryan was that his plan would work. It's true that Bo isn't fond of work, but on the other hand he really enjoys beating up guys who are smaller than him.

At lunchtime, I found out that I'd been right. Bryan slumped into the chair across from me, took a deep breath, and told me the bad news.

"He says no way he's letting you off for one week of homework. And he wouldn't go for two weeks either."

I shoved my sandwich away and waited for the rest of it.

"He says the rest of the semester."

I opened my mouth to protest and barely caught myself in time to cut off my first word, which came out like a squeaky "aw." Bryan laughed and said I sounded like a crow. Big help.

The rest of the semester was more than two months! There was *no way* I was doing Bo Werner's homework for that long. I shook my head "no."

"It's your call, dude, but you know he's really going to let you have it."

I shrugged to show that I didn't care but the truth was I was pretty scared. I'd been in fights before, but only a few times and only because I was really mad when they were happening. I knew I couldn't summon up enough anger to have it count for anything in a fight against Bo.

I kept telling myself that it wasn't that big of a deal. So, I'd get punched a few times, maybe kicked once or twice, and it'd be over. I'd have a couple of bruises and be sore for a while and that would be the end of it.

It also occurred to me that thinking about it wasn't going to help. Not that this was one of those things that are worse when you think about them than when they happen, but I still thought I might just as well get it over with.

So, to keep from stretching the whole thing out, I gave Bryan a note to give to Bo. It told him that I'd be at Patter's Peak Park, which is about a five minute walk from my place, right after school. I almost wrote something about settling the score, but then I decided there was no sense in putting on the big dramatic tough guy act. It would only make me look more foolish when I got flattened.

Sending off the note gave me a strange sense of relief. Somehow, I was able to focus on the idea of it almost being over with instead of how much blood I might be missing afterward.

It took about four minutes for word of my upcoming thrashing to race through the school and before the first class of the afternoon was over I was getting the expected whispers. Most of them were from guys who were just as scared of Bo as I was. They basically offered suggestions on how I could beat him. Unfortunately, a lot of them involved a target that I wasn't particularly keen to touch. And anyway, sinking to Bo's level wouldn't mean winning — he'd just come after me again some other time.

A few girls came up to me too, but they weren't quite as single-minded as the guys. Peggy Ashton and Terri Dorsey both told me (in oddly excited whispers) that they thought I was *so* brave, though how getting beat up equates to courage wasn't clear to me.

Erica Spears sidled up to me with a quick commentary on how stupid and barbaric fighting is while we walked to English class. Ruby Hawkins clutched the cross she wears around her neck pretty well every day and told me she was praying for me.

And Mira Travis, of course, batted her dumb eyes and, with trembling lips, said she would "be there for me" — whatever *that* was supposed to accomplish.

Of course, I couldn't answer anybody, and it struck me that they might as well have all stayed quiet too, since nothing anyone had said had been of any particular value.

Then, during English class, Mr. Furlong managed to distract me from thoughts of the fight by bringing up the speeches. He went over a few points, talked about finding topics for those who hadn't yet settled on anything, and then he got to me.

"In your case," he said, standing over my desk, "I suppose we'll need to have an alternative — in the event that you maintain your protest of silence throughout the speech deliveries."

I had a fleeting thought that at least the plan was paying off, even if it had brought a lot of trouble I hadn't counted on. Then he continued.

"Your reason for the protest would, of course, be the perfect topic for you to speak on, so it seems sensible for you to go with that."

I must have looked confused (and probably panicked) at that. He explained.

"Not for a speech, of course, if it turns out you're unable to deliver one. I thought perhaps an essay on the subject. Something around a thousand words, though you can have more if necessary."

A *thousand* words? I could hardly manage two or three hundred words for essay assignments. There was no way I was going to be able to come up with a thousand words on a subject I knew nothing about.

"So, Griffin, does that sound like a fair substitution to you?"

What could I do? I nodded my head miserably, wondering how such a simple idea had turned into this complicated mess: a thousand word essay and the fact that I was about to get creamed by the school bully hardly seemed like a fair trade for avoiding a few minutes of humiliation.

I tried to convince myself it was worth it. In a couple of weeks the speeches would be over with, I could start talking again, and everything would be back to normal.

But first, I had to get the fight with Bo behind me.

CHAPTER EIGHT

Bryan walked with me, eyes downcast and face as gloomy as if *he* was the one about to face Bo's fists. For once, he didn't have much to say — besides reminding me a couple of times that I didn't have to go through with it. I could tell he didn't actually think I was going to be talked out of it because he didn't put much effort into persuading me. We both knew there really wasn't anything else I could do.

As we turned the corner to the park we could see that a crowd was already gathering. As I got close enough to make out who was there, I saw that at least some of the kids were friends of mine.

Bo's henchmen were there too, off to the side of the main group, forming a circle. I knew he would be in the centre of the ring and that the guys around him would be coaching him. I also knew that they couldn't come up with an original thought among the lot of them, so it would all be your basic dirty-fighting advice.

Bryan saw them, too. "Keep the boys covered," he said. His voice was flat; his face showed nothing.

There was nothing to say to that. I just nodded.

The circle opened and Bo emerged from the parted bodies. He got rid of his jacket, peeling it off slowly, and stood there — unbelievably — in a tank top. Not your standard winter wear, and it almost made me laugh, although I don't think that was the intended effect. He'd been wearing a sweatshirt earlier in the day and hadn't had time to go home and change, so I figured he'd been wearing it under the sweat, or maybe he'd had it in his locker for gym.

He was pumped and I realized his goons had been shielding him while he did some push-ups or something to get those muscles bulging. That in itself wasn't particularly scary to me. After all, I already knew he was a lot bigger and stronger than me.

What *was* kind of frightening was the look in his eyes. They were lit up and darting around — sort of wild — taking in the crowd's reaction, feeding on the bloodlust that always hangs in the air at a fight.

Whispers ran through the crowd, gaining volume as the excitement mounted. My heart sank a little knowing that, while some of them would honestly like to see me win, they were all more or less animated by the thought of blood, bruises, and even broken bones.

In the end, anyone's would do.

Of course, there was no question as to who would be

left standing at the end of *this* match. Earlier, I'd asked Bryan to check out the betting pool Glen Massey had going and give me the details. He'd done that and apparently you could bet on how many punches it took me to go down (and stay there) in the first minute. For those who thought I'd make it past the minute, time slots were sold in five-second increments.

The single option for anyone foolish enough to bet on me was simple: Maxwell to win. No time, no number of punches, and (when Bryan had looked into it) no bets.

Glen was there with a stopwatch and a small booklet that held details of the bets. He took twenty-five percent of the money (administration fees, he said) anytime he ran a pool. It meant nothing to him who won or when.

Reggie Bertrand was there, too — naturally. He made a fool of himself trying to make eye contact with me, no doubt to remind me to take a dive and win him the pool. I was careful to let my eyes wander in his general direction without looking right at him, which drove him to more and more obvious gestures and facial distortions.

I was surprised that no one realized he was trying to send me a signal. I guess Reggie is so strange that everyone just dismissed the contortions as part of his normal weirdness.

Or maybe no one noticed because they were all watching Bo, who had taken a few steps toward me and then paused for the big dramatic build-up. I knew he'd soak up some of the tension in the air even as it grew and swelled to a fever.

Meanwhile, the normal thing for someone facing him would be to stand there, rooted to the spot, and try not to show too much fear. That didn't appeal to me much and besides, I was strung so tight at that moment I thought I might snap and do something really foolish. Like run.

So, instead of chancing it, I decided to take his moment from him. It might be the only victory I'd get, but it suddenly became more important than anything else.

I started toward him, taking even steps, looking straight at him. It startled him so much that I swear I saw a flash of fear cross his face. Maybe it was only uncertainty, but whatever it was, for that split second Bo was shaken by my move.

A murmur ran through the crowd, a sound of surprise and wonder. The skinny kid walking steadily toward the certain winner was something they'd never expected, and I felt a rush of pride that strengthened my knees enough to take me the final few steps.

I lifted my chin and smiled right at Bo. Another flicker of doubt. It was all I needed. I felt as though I'd won something bigger than the fight itself.

"You got this coming!" Bo said, breaking the silence that had fallen on the group. "You got to learn not to be disrespectin' Bo Werner."

I smiled again.

"I guess you need that smile wiped off for you," he

said. But there was no force or determination in his voice.

"Put your hands up and fight like a man!" he said, yelling.

I stood, relaxed, in front of him; arms down, chin up, smile in place. Suddenly, a voice in the crowd, just barely audible, said, "Griffin."

The chant was almost instant. "Griffin! Griffin! Griffin!" They made a song of it, while confusion and uncertainty grew on Bo's face. Then it turned to anger and the moment was over.

The first punch hit me solidly on the left shoulder, driving me back a step. I was surprised how much it hurt, but I tried not to let that show on my face. I shook it off.

Among the voices in the crowd, I heard Reggie Bertrand shout out a protest.

"That doesn't count!"

I darted a glance at him. His expression, wild and desperate with the thought that his guaranteed win was slipping away, actually made me laugh.

As my eyes cut back to Bo I saw that he'd been about to come at me, but had frozen in mid-step at the bizarre sight of me laughing. Before he could advance, I stepped forward again and waited.

Thwack! His knuckles connected with my ribs, taking the wind out of me. I sucked hard, trying to get in air.

"Fight back!" he yelled, following with a right to my

stomach. Bo isn't smart at much, but he knows a few things about fighting and I could see he was making this last.

He could have just punched me in the face a few times and gotten the whole thing over with, but he was saving it, preferring to toy with me. Lots of guys get in fights, but most of them don't drag it out, enjoying every minute of making someone suffer. That takes a certain kind of creep — like Bo.

Because he wasn't going for the quick win I knew that by the time he went for my face I wouldn't have enough left in me to dodge him, supposing I tried to.

The chants had stopped pretty fast and within a minute or two the only sounds coming from the crowd were yells from Bo's gang. Mostly, "Kill him!" Talk about original.

It didn't take long before my ribs and sides felt like they were on fire with pain. I could hardly catch my breath between blows and I knew I couldn't take much more.

It wasn't worth it.

The thought struck me that all I had to do to make it stop was say "uncle." A single word and it would be over. So what if it meant this was all for nothing? So what if I had to give a speech? The only thing that mattered was making the pain stop.

Relief flooded over me as I made the decision to do it, to give in.

"Uncle." Except, when I opened my mouth to say it, nothing came out. I tried again. Squat. On the third attempt Bo's fist drove the breath out of me and I folded over in agony.

Twice more I struggled to get the word out; twice more I failed.

It blurred after that. I lost count of how many punches he landed before he started on my face but once he started connecting there, it was just a matter of letting myself be sucked into the nauseating grey-black vortex that was rushing toward me.

When I opened my eyes it was to a circle of faces hovering over me. I heard my name and I heard someone say to stand back and give me some air. That might have been Bryan, but I'm not sure because it all blurred and then faded to black again.

The next time I drifted back up I stayed awake, though it was a few minutes before I could get to my feet. I staggered a few steps and almost fell. Bryan grabbed an arm and held on until he was convinced I wasn't going to fall over.

As the crowd drifted off, we slowly made our way away from the park and along the street toward my place. When we reached it, I signalled Bryan to go. He'd made sure I got home okay, but it would be way beyond the call of friendship for him to stay and face the music with me.

He hesitated, but the thought of escape was too appealing for any sane person to turn down. Just before he turned to leave, he cleared his throat like he was going to say something, but in the end he just shook his head like something was puzzling him. Then he walked away.

I let him clear the yard before turning the doorknob and going inside.

CHAPTER NINE

I probably don't have to tell you that my mother wigged out when she saw my face, which didn't actually look as bad as I expected it to. Luckily, it didn't seem to occur to her that I might be hurt somewhere else, or she'd have probably dragged me to the hospital.

"What happened?" she demanded while she draped a cold, wet cloth on my face and started making cold packs by wrapping ice cubes from the freezer in some small towels.

I didn't answer her question, of course, which only made her freak more.

"Yes, yes, I know you're not talking," she said impatiently. "But this is different. You can certainly make an exception for something like this."

I shook my head and made writing motions in the air while I tried to get my brain to focus on a cover story. Mom didn't look happy but she went and got a notepad and pen. She slid the pad in front of me on the table and thwacked the pen down with a motion that told me there wasn't going to be any negotiating. She was *going* to get a full explanation and that was all there was to it.

I wrote slowly, forming the story as I scrawled words onto the page. An argument that got out of control, exploded into a fight ... it wouldn't happen again. I added that everything had worked out afterward — and that we'd even shaken hands. Right.

The single truth in what I wrote was Bo's name and that was only because it was possible she'd hear it mentioned by someone else — or more accurately, either Kellie or Nicole would hear it from someone else and blab it to her.

Mom read over my shoulder, went through it twice, and then sat down at the table with pursed lips. She leaned forward, tapping a pink fingernail on the hard surface.

"I don't like this one bit, Griffin," she said. "You can't go around losing your temper and getting into fistfights like this ... you could get badly hurt. Besides, violence never solves anything."

I sat with the pen held loosely in my hand, wondering if she was expecting some kind of answer.

"You're going to have some bruises," she said after a pause. "Even with the ice, there's already some swelling and discolouration."

You should see my chest and gut, I thought.

Mom sighed. It looked like she was trying to think of something else to say and just couldn't come up with anything. I could see she was upset, but not as much as I'd expected, which was a relief. After a few more minutes she stood up, checked under the ice packs she'd made for me, and then leaned down and kissed me on the top of the head.

"It's not like you to get into fights," she said, touching my hair lightly. "It upsets me. You could have been hurt much worse, you know, and I ... well, I just hope it won't happen again."

I made an effort, numb face and all, to give her a reassuring smile, but for some reason that made her cover her mouth and rush out of the room. I knew she was crying and that bothered me more than if she'd yelled at me and grounded me, or whatever.

"What happened to *you?*"

I turned to see Kellie standing there, hands on her hips, face twisted in distaste. She took a step closer, peering at me like I had fungus growing on my face.

It hit me that she'd find out the truth and if she figured out I'd covered it up with Mom she'd burn the soles off her shoes in her haste to rat me out. I knew I should try to think of some way to keep that from happening but my head hurt, I couldn't think clearly, and at that moment I couldn't summon the energy to care.

"You're missing a spot," she said, coming closer. She reached out and slid one of the cloths I was holding against my face up an inch or so. Then she swatted me lightly on the top of the head and called me a doofus.

I suppose that was to let me know she wasn't getting soft on me.

A wave of queasiness hit me then, and I made my way to the bathroom and sat on the edge of the tub facing the toilet. After a couple of minutes of nothing happening I decided to lie down and see if it would pass.

In my room and flat out on the bed a minute later I found I suddenly felt weak and exhausted. I closed my eyes, still holding the cloths on the bruises. Trails of water slid down the sides of my head as the ice melted and I remember thinking maybe I should put something underneath me so my pillow wouldn't get soaked. Thinking about it was as far as I got. I couldn't summon the energy to move.

I ran through the whole fight scene in my head, and then I thought about the fact that I'd tried to speak — to save myself — and hadn't been able to. Wondering why my voice had failed me at that exact moment, I thought it would be a good idea to check it out then.

I tried to speak.

Nothing.

I tried and tried and tried but every attempt was the same.

I'd lost the ability to talk!

As scary as that was, my need to rest overcame it. The next thing I knew I was waking up. My hands were flopped beside me and the cloths they'd held were gone except for one lying across my forehead.

My room was dark. Someone had closed the blinds and turned out the light.

I could hear voices in the other room, along with the sounds of knives and forks clinking against plates. That made me realize I was hungry, but the thought of getting up and going to the kitchen was more than I could manage.

As I woke up more and my eyes adjusted to the dark, I realized that there was someone sitting beside my bed. I turned toward the dark figure and was startled to make out my father's shape.

"Hey," he said softly, seeing that I'd noticed him. "How are you feeling?"

I lifted a hand and gave it a back-and-forth wave.

"So-so, huh? I'm guessing that it'll hurt for a few days — not much you can do about that." A long pause and then, "I guess you don't want to add anything to what you told your mother?"

I shook my head "no" without looking at him.

He stood up and came a few steps closer. "You having trouble with anyone, Son? Anything that this didn't settle?"

I shook my head "no" for a second time, but stopped when the nausea started up again.

"All right then," he said. He hesitated just a little. "You can come to me ... if you find yourself in any kind of mess. I hope you know that, Griffin."

I nodded, careful not to move my head too rapidly.

That seemed to satisfy him. He patted my shoulder and cleared his throat. "I can bring you some supper if you want."

I was tempted to say "yes" but just as I was about to answer I remembered how Mom had left the kitchen in tears earlier. So, instead, I pushed myself to a sitting position and swung my legs off the bed to show Dad I was getting up.

First stop was the bathroom where I drained the old dragon and then washed up and splashed water on my face. It didn't look as bad as I'd expected, though I knew the bruising would get worse by the next day. My left eye was swollen with a dark circle under it and both cheeks were puffy and darkening, but there were no cuts and my mouth was, miraculously, untouched.

The main thing was that it was over. I congratulated myself on not caving over the homework deal Bo had wanted. A little pain for a few days had to be better than being a sap for the rest of the semester.

Dad and I went to the kitchen then and dished up plates. By the time I'd eaten a piece of chicken and a baked potato (I skipped the whipped turnip and no one even said a word) my stomach had settled and I felt a lot better.

Even Mom did okay. Except for a couple of choked sobs, which she swallowed back quickly, she managed to act like everything was perfectly normal.

CHAPTER TEN

Mom suggested that I might want to skip school the next day, but I told her I was fine. There was no way I was going to give Bo the satisfaction of thinking he'd hurt me bad enough to keep me home, even for one day.

Her next idea was even worse.

"Why don't I just put a little cover stick on those bruises?" she said, just as Bryan arrived to walk to school with me.

I had no idea what cover stick even was. I made some gestures to that effect and I guess I was getting better at making myself understood because she got it right away.

"Cover stick? It's to hide things like blemishes or dark lines under your eyes, but it should work to conceal your bruises."

Horrified, I realized she was talking about putting *makeup* on me. As if. I shook my head and took a couple of steps backward, just in case. I was making sure I had a clear escape route. Mom can come at you sometimes when she gets something in her head.

She didn't, though. She sighed and then came over all teary-eyed, kissed me right in front of Bryan, and told me to watch myself and to stay out of trouble.

"Your mom must think you're quite the renegade outlaw," Bryan commented as we headed down the street. "Does she know why you got beat up?"

I gave him a look that said, "What kind of question is that?"

"Easy, dude. I didn't mean you told her. I just thought maybe one of your sisters said something."

I relaxed but it made me realize how tensed up I'd been. It also hit me that it really didn't have much to do with what Bryan had said. I just wasn't looking forward to facing everybody, knowing they'd all be whispering about how I got creamed.

So, it was a surprise to get near the school and find out the general reaction wasn't what I'd expected. Junior Gallagher was the first one to speak.

"Hey, Griffin! We were just talking about you!"

"Yo! You the *man*, bro," said Efrain Dawson.

"Yeah, that was awesome, Griff!" said Evan Scott.

"Yeah, *awesome*," agreed Rob Wheeler.

"*You* weren't even *there*," Evan said to him.

Rob and Evan are both in foster care and live with some other kids in a group home called Dunlap Place. Evan has been in some trouble, but he's really an all right guy. Rob's a bit harder to take. Just about anything that comes out of his mouth is likely a lie, if you know the type.

"I *was so* there," he said, right on schedule. The rest of us did what we usually do and just ignored him.

By then a lot of other guys were gathering around, congratulating me, whacking me on the back, telling me I had real guts and stuff like that. It wasn't exactly the kind of reaction I'd been expecting, considering that I'd ended the fight flat on my butt.

"You showed him!" This comment came from Geoff Lancaster, who'd once asked me if I'd put in a good word for him with Kellie. (I'd said I would but of course I hadn't had the slightest intention. The guy didn't know the humiliation I'd spared him.)

I passed Reggie Bertrand in the hall (actually, it looked like he was waiting for me to go by) and as I did he muttered something resentful about how I wouldn't have gotten beat up if I'd just listened to him.

I stopped and backtracked a couple of steps, squared off, and looked him right in the eye. Stood there and stared until he looked away. I can't be sure, since no words were exchanged, but I think he got the message.

I heard it all day. Guys came up and congratulated me and said stuff about how brave I'd been. It was like *I'd* won the fight.

The guys were one thing, but the girls were another story. The normal girls were okay, but it seemed like the weirdoes were acting creepier than ever.

Mira came up to me between second and third period and started saying something stupid about true courage or some such slop, and then, halfway through, she got all choked up, clapped both hands over her mouth and took off like someone was chasing her.

By the end of the school day I was ready to get away from everyone — whether they were treating me like a hero or not. It was way too much attention for a guy like me to handle.

Bryan and I walked to his place and this time we had the place to ourselves. He grabbed some brownies and milk and we sat at the kitchen island to eat.

"So!" he said, "I guess you're glad that's over with."

I nodded.

"Hey, it's cool," he said, "there's no one else here. You can go ahead and talk."

I managed to get out something that sounded like "Oi!" but that was it. Then I flapped my mouth a couple more times. Not a sound.

"*What* is the *matter* with you?" he asked.

I frowned and raised my eyebrows questioningly and pointed to my throat.

Bryan stared for a minute, but he got the message. Then he was quiet for a bit, thinking it through. It didn't take him long to come up with an idea.

"Must be like, psychosomatic," he said, nodding wisely. "Probably your conscience is bugging you. You know, because you're being, like, a total fraud."

I must not have looked too pleased at that because he hastened to add, "Not that that's a *bad* thing. I mean, you're just doing what you have to do. But your head might be messing with your voice."

I ripped a sheet of paper out of a binder from my backpack and wrote, "How long can this psycho stuff last?"

"I dunno. Maybe a few days," he said. "I think for it to be longer — like years or something — you'd probably have to be a lot more complex than you are. I mean, face it, Griff, you're not that deep. Besides, a thing like this would hardly ever be permanent."

That was when I put my hand up to stop him before he could say anything *else* to make me feel better.

At home a bit later everyone went out of their way to be nice to me. Mom and Dad ... well, you'd kind of expect that from them, but not the girls, so having them treat me like a human being was a surprise. Leah patted my arm and gave me this weird, goofy smile. I rubbed the top of her head to let her know that I knew what she meant.

Nicole managed to forget how she'd acted when I'd first stopped talking, and went on and on about how she'd been behind me from the start and was really proud of what I was doing. (I don't know if anyone besides me noticed her amnesia, but no one said anything to her.)

The really big shock was Kellie. She didn't once call me a reject or moron or anything all through supper, which is pretty unusual for her. She even passed me the salt when I was trying to signal for gravy, and I was so stunned that I salted my potatoes and ate them dry.

I turned it all over in my head as I drifted off to sleep that night — the way everyone was acting as if I was some kind of hero. It might have felt really good, except I knew I didn't deserve it. All I'd done was hide how scared I was while I was getting beat up.

And nobody but me knew that I'd tried to give up.

Chapter Eleven

The buzz over the fight had died down by Friday but I had other things on my mind by then anyway.

First off, my folks were starting to get impatient with the fact that I didn't have a plan. And, apparently, so were some of my teachers. Mom told me that the school had called them to ask just what my goal was in this whole thing and how long it was expected to go on.

Coming up with answers to their questions was getting harder and harder and I knew I couldn't hold them off with vague notes much longer. "I've got it under control" and "It won't be long now" weren't working anymore. I was starting to worry that I was going to have to come up with a concrete plan, though I was still hoping I could stall everyone until after the speeches were done.

If I could do that, then I was home free. There would be an easy out for me when it was safe for me to start talking again: I'd just say I hadn't been able to come up with a good enough plan and so I was forced to quit.

Another big problem was Furlong's essay assignment. I knew I needed to spend the weekend working on the thousand-word essay. That was bad enough, but the seriously bad news came when I scribbled a note about it to Bryan at lunchtime.

"Oh, yeah. I heard Furlong assigning that to you. Sorry, man, but I'm not going to be able to help this weekend. We're going to my grandmother's place, remember?"

I'd completely forgotten about that, though Bryan had mentioned it earlier in the week. He and his parents have spent the weekend with his grandmother every couple of months since his grandfather died a few years ago.

I wrote again and passed him the page.

"Send you stuff by e-mail?" His face told me it wasn't going to be good news even before he spoke. "My grandmother doesn't have the internet. She doesn't even have a computer. I'm afraid you're on your own this time, Griff. But don't worry, I'll show you where to go to get started."

He paused for a second, which is all he ever needs to drag up information. "Some of the stuff I found was on the Amnesty International site. Just search through their news stories and look for links to articles about your soldiers."

My soldiers.

I trudged home dejectedly and, as I'd done for the past few days, I took a path that went through the yard of an old abandoned house. It was no shorter, and it meant getting my pants wet in the snow, but I needed the privacy.

As soon as I was past the back corner of the empty house (and well hidden by the spruce and cedar trees that edged the property) I cleared my throat and tried to speak.

Nothing. Not a sound. Not even a squeak.

Reaching into my backpack, I pulled out a bottle of water that I'd grabbed that morning for this very reason. Since the fight, when I'd tried to talk but couldn't, I'd got thinking that maybe my throat had, I dunno, seized up or something. Maybe it was like an engine and it had stopped working from not being used. It seemed reasonable that maybe if I just wet my throat a little, things would start to work again.

I took a couple of big gulps and tried again.

Nothing.

At least I'd been able to make *some* kind of sound when I'd tried to talk to Bryan. Now, I was down to pure, absolute silence.

Determined not to give up, I poured more water in and gargled, kind of making sure my throat was good and moistened. After I'd spit that out, I took another drink. I tried again.

Nothing.

And as hard as I tried not to think of it, there was only one thought in my head: What if I could never talk again?

A hot, panicky feeling ran through me, making me sweat in spite of the cold. It was the kind of feeling I'd get when I was a little kid and my mom caught me in the act of doing something bad.

I tried to calm myself down by thinking of what Bryan had said and hoping he was right. But I couldn't get rid of the thought that Bryan, brilliant or not, is just a kid like me. He could be totally wrong.

I wasn't quite ready to give up for the day, though, so I ran through a list of words I'd come up with in class that afternoon. I'd got to thinking that certain letters or sounds might be harder to make than others, and maybe I'd been trying to start on the wrong ones.

My list included words I figured might be the easiest to say. Bee. Moo. No. Shoe. Sea.

I mouthed them all. Not a sound.

I sighed, and even that seemed to come out quieter than usual. I remembered Bryan telling me that the worst thing I could do was obsess over it. He swore that would only make it worse.

So I tried to distract myself and think of other things. I don't know if you've ever tried that, but it's almost im-possible to make yourself *not* think about something. It was a relief to get home and to find something that took my mind off it — at least a bit.

Ariel was there with Kellie.

"Ariel is sleeping over," Kellie told me the second she could grab me aside without anyone hearing. "And one thing we don't need is a reject lurking around us being all quiet and weird. So keep out of our way."

At least some things were back to normal.

I just shrugged. I mean, it's not like I go out of my way to be around Ariel; it's just that it works out like that sometimes when she's over. Like, they might be watching something on TV that I really want to see. Is that a crime?

One time they were putting on some outfits, trying to decide what to wear to the show, and Ariel asked me to give them a *guy's point of view* on the different combinations. So, I know that it's only Kellie who doesn't want me around.

But with a thousand-word essay to write and only a couple of days to get it done, I didn't have time to hang out with them even if I wanted to.

Nicole was on the computer, chatting with someone on Messenger, when I went into the den. She looked annoyed when I sat down in the chair behind her and she kept moving to shield the screen so I couldn't see what she was writing. Like I cared.

"Uh, Griff," she said after a minute, "I'd kind of like some privacy here."

I picked up a magazine and flipped through it, like I thought that would satisfy her. She dropped a few more hints designed to make me leave, but I played dumb and just kept pretending to cooperate by reading, moving to another seat, and fumbling with an old magic knot puzzle.

The thing about Nicole is she's always telling Kellie not to be so bossy, unladylike, pushy, hateful, and on and on. That makes it kind of hard for her to act the same way, and she hardly ever tells me what to do, even when she really wants to.

Eventually, she gave up and left the room. I slid into the computer seat right away, just in case. We only have one computer and it's not always easy to get a turn on it.

I had to think for a few minutes about the name of the site Bryan had mentioned. It finally came to me: Amnesty International.

I sure hoped they had lots of information. As long as I found enough stuff to put together this ridiculously long essay, I was okay.

The possibility flashed through my head that maybe Mr. Furlong was suspicious and had given me the assignment as some kind of test. Or to teach me a lesson. But he'd seemed sincere when he talked to me about it, like he was just giving me an option to kind of support what I was doing.

And he'd actually said I could make it longer if I needed to. There'd been no sign of a smirk or anything on his face when he made that crazy comment, so I was pretty sure he bought the whole story. He probably thought I'd researched it and knew all about the whole thing. Otherwise, why would I be doing the protest?

Either way, I had a lot of work ahead of me!

Chapter Twelve

It was no problem finding the site Bryan had told me to look up, and after typing in a few keywords I found myself with more links than I could even *read* in a weekend, much less write about. The problem was going to be where to start.

I remembered a teacher telling us that statistics can be a good way to open an essay, so I got looking through a few pages for numbers.

It didn't take long to find some. I have to admit I was shocked when I read that *two million* children had been killed in combat in the last ten years. I hadn't expected that. I jotted the number down, then stared at it for a minute.

I remembered something my dad had told me one time. He said that if a number is too big, it doesn't mean anything to people — that a number only really means something to you if you can relate to it.

So, I decided to break it down — make it mean something. I'm not great at doing math in my head, but even

I knew that two million in ten years worked out to two hundred thousand in one year.

Still too big. I got out my calculator and divided the two hundred thousand by 365. The number that came back was 548, only that seemed like a lot. I thought maybe I'd hit too many zeroes or something, so I did it over. It was right.

I jotted down 548.

As I stared at the number, it suddenly hit me that there are around 550 kids at my school, almost exactly the number of kids who were being wiped out in warfare every day of the year. A whole school full of kids. Dead. Every day.

I wrote it down. *Every day, almost five hundred and fifty children die fighting in wars.*

A thought struck me and I grabbed a yearbook and flipped it open to the inside cover, where they have one of those big pictures with all the students standing out in front of the school. The kind where you can't tell who's who.

I looked at it for a couple of minutes and tried to picture all of them — all of us, actually — wiped out. The thought made me cold.

And that would just be in *one* day. There had been that many deaths *every day for the last ten years*. It was like wiping out more than *thirty-five hundred* schools.

You know, when there are acts of terrorism, or someone flips out and starts shooting people, everybody talks about it for weeks. And those things are awful — no question — but it doesn't even come close to being as bad as that many *kids* fighting and dying in battle every year — or even every day.

So, how come we don't hear about it? You'd think it would be the most talked about thing on the planet.

I shoved back the questions that were running through my head and got back to work.

Every site and organization I looked at seemed to lead to more. After browsing around for a while I clicked on a link called "Children and War" and started reading.

More shocking numbers! Throughout the world, over 300,000 kids under eighteen, with many as young as ten — and even younger — were being forced to fight as soldiers.

Refusing wasn't an option, either. There was no choice for these kids. The only hope they had was to somehow get away, but if they got caught trying to escape they'd be killed.

The next page described how they're forced into cooperation. They were abused in every possible way — sexually, physically, and emotionally. From what I understood, beating them, scaring them half to death, making them do terrible things — all of this helped their captors turn them into obedient and ruthless killers.

If the 300,000 figure was right, then this was happening to more than a quarter of a million kids. But the casualty rates among child soldiers are really high, which got me thinking: if that was true, there must be more kids being dragged into the terror every day.

I started reading in earnest, going from page to page, scribbling down facts and sometimes printing out pages.

Travelling from link to link I found stories told by the kids themselves. Like this one from Susan, a thirteen-year-old kid on a site called "Human Rights Watch":

One boy tried to escape, but he was caught. They made him eat a mouthful of red pepper, and five people were beating him. His hands were tied, and then they made us, the other new captives, kill him with a stick. I felt sick. I knew this boy from before. We were from the same village. I refused to kill him and they told me they would shoot me. They pointed a gun at me, so I had to do it. The boy was asking me, "Why are you doing this?" I said I had no choice. After we killed him, they made us smear his blood on our arms. I felt dizzy. There was another dead body nearby, and I could smell the body. I felt so sick. They said we had to do this so we would not fear death and so we would not try to escape.

I feel so bad about the things that I did.... It disturbs me so much — that I inflicted death on other people.... When I go home I must do some traditional rites because I have killed. I

must perform these rites and cleanse myself. I
still dream about the boy from my village who I
killed. I see him in my dreams, and he is talking
to me and saying I killed him for nothing, and
I am crying.

A feeling crawled up my back when I read that and I wanted
to stop, but there were many stories from the child soldiers
and it was like I had no choice. I had to keep reading.

I was hoping at least that what the girl named Susan
said was unusual — something that didn't normally
happen — but no. A lot of the kids talked about being
forced to kill other kids — mostly for trying to escape.

What kinds of monsters would kidnap children and
then make them hurt, *or kill*, their own families, friends,
and neighbours? How could you do that to *anyone*, least
of all a little kid?

I found some pictures of a few of the kids and looked
hard at them. It seemed that there was something simi-
lar in their faces. It took me a minute to figure it out but
when I did it seemed obvious.

The eyes were all vacant, like someone had gotten
inside and cut out the part of them that feels or cares.
They had the kind of emptiness in their expressions
that said no matter what anyone did to them now, it
wouldn't matter.

Some of them looked at least a couple of years
younger than I am.

Some kids got killed because their feet swelled up and they couldn't walk anymore, others because they couldn't carry stuff that was too heavy for them. It was hard to picture that — dying because your feet got swollen or you weren't strong enough to handle the load someone forced on you.

By the time I'd finished reading the first-hand accounts from the children whose words were recorded in "The Scars of Death" on the Human Rights Watch site I couldn't stand to go any further that night.

I closed all the files and looked at my notes. I hadn't written much and what I *had* jotted down seemed to be missing something. Even though I'd only been reading most of the time I suddenly felt really, really tired.

CHAPTER THIRTEEN

First thing Saturday morning I got back to doing research, printing pages, gathering notes, and trying to put things in some kind of order. That was a lot harder than you'd think, because it seemed every link I checked out led me to more and more sites.

I made a list of the different organizations I'd discovered that were trying to do something about kids being forced to fight in wars. In just a few hours, I'd found:

- Amnesty International (with branches in lots of countries)
- The Coalition to Stop the Use of Child Soldiers
- Child Soldiers: Giving a Voice to Children Affected by War
- War Child
- Human Rights Watch
- International Save the Children Alliance

There were other groups, too, that were working on the problem in specific countries, but I didn't write them down because there were too many.

Then, I found a site that talked about a new draft resolution from the United Nations. I'd heard of the UN before but I really had no idea what it was. It only took a few minutes to find out that it's a worldwide organization that looks out for human rights.

I browsed around a bit more and found that the UN had a page just about children's rights.

I clicked the link and found a write-up along with more links on the side. Reading through it, I saw that the UN had had a Convention on the Rights of the Child back in 1989.

It was kind of cool to know that this huge organization had a special thing for kids. Not just some kids, either. Apparently, every child, everywhere, was covered by this thing.

I jotted down: *United Nations Convention on the Rights of the Child, 1989. No matter who you are and no matter where you are, all children (under 18) everywhere have fundamental rights that are protected by international law.*

There was a logo in the right margin of the online page with a kid jumping rope and the words "No exceptions" beside him.

I knew what *that* meant. My Science teacher last year used it all the time to threaten us about how we'd get zeroes if we didn't have projects passed in on time. She'd get all fierce looking and tap her pointer on the desk and do her best to let us know she meant business. Only, she did make exceptions, if you were sick or something.

But I figured if a big, powerful organization like the UN said "no exceptions," they meant it.

I read the whole page about children's rights again, then checked out a couple of the links. I was getting a good feeling from it — kind of important. Like all kids — even me — really matter to these guys.

A little more exploring and I found ODS — a place where you can read and print out official documents from the UN. I decided to see what they were doing to help these kids.

I printed the draft resolution and started reading. It seemed that the UN was still paying close attention to the subject. The document started out by reviewing what had been going on and stressing how unacceptable it was. Then there was a lot of stuff about a monitoring-and-reporting plan, but I couldn't figure out what they were going to do once that was finished.

After all the stuff about protecting kids, how did it fit with what I'd learned yesterday? I bet the kids who were dying every day wouldn't be too impressed with all the fancy words and ideas. Still, it had to mean something.

I'd just finished making a bunch of notes about the UN stuff when Mom appeared in the doorway.

"There's a call for you," she said, holding up the cordless phone. "It's Bryan, and he knows you can't talk, but he said he has something to tell you. He said to tell you to tap the mouthpiece so he'll know you're there."

I took the phone and tapped as she'd instructed.

"Hey, dude! I just had a great idea for your essay!" He paused. "Uh, tap twice if you heard that."

I did and he went on. "You can write this down if you want. Tap once anytime you want me to pause.

"For an opening line, you definitely want to start with a tear-jerker. Okay, here it is: Picture yourself sitting with your family, sharing a meal, talking about everyday things, when suddenly your door is kicked open and men with guns rush in. Instantly, screaming and shouting, fear and panic fill the air around you. Imagine the terror and hopelessness you feel as these men grab you and your siblings and force you to go with them.

"As they shove you out the door, you can hear your mother's wails and your father's helpless protests. As you are led away you know that these may be the last sights and sounds you will ever have of your home and parents. At twelve years of age, you have just been 'recruited' into the army."

I'd been writing down what he said when he started, but I'd stopped halfway through. Something about it was bothering me, though I didn't know what or why. I knew Bryan was trying to help out, but for some reason there was this anger building up inside me.

"So, I guess that's it then," he said. His voice had kind of trailed off, which I guess is natural since he was the only one talking. "Anyway, go ahead and use that to start your essay if you want."

Of course, he assumed I'd want to. It was a good beginning. But I knew I wasn't going to use it.

"Well, I gotta get going," Bryan said then, but he paused for a few seconds before hanging up.

I clicked off the phone and took it back to the charger in the living room, grabbed a banana and a glass of water from the kitchen, and went back to the computer.

I spent almost the whole day Saturday and more than half the day Sunday doing research, printing pages, making notes, and trying to get an outline together for my essay. When I finally stopped I had more than enough material but I felt like I'd hardly scratched the surface.

My head and stomach both hurt by the time I'd started to write the actual essay. By bedtime Sunday night I'd spent the entire weekend working on it, but at least I had a rough draft done and could see the light at the end of the tunnel.

As I fell asleep that night I thought how glad I'd be to have it finished. I could hardly wait to put the whole thing behind me.

Only, as tired as I was, I kept waking up. All through the night, over and over, I dreamt about those kids standing in front of me, staring through me with their blank eyes.

And in every dream I asked them why their eyes were so empty. I tried to shake them, to wake them from their trance-like states, only when I did, they toppled over.

Their eyes were telling me something I didn't want to know. Those kids were already dead.

CHAPTER FOURTEEN

Monday was my tenth day of silence and, to be honest, it was starting to feel pretty comfortable. Except for the worry about when (I tried not to dwell on the "if") I was going to be able to talk again, I'd realized there were some unexpected benefits to my silence.

The most obvious one was that teachers didn't call on me in class. I have to admit that not all of them were enthusiastic about the situation, though a couple clearly thought it was a great thing. The others (I could tell) were tolerating it impatiently, just waiting for the end of the foolishness.

It was funny how I got more and more able to "hear" things even when nothing was said. It was like my own silence had given me the ability to read the meanings *behind* what other people said and did. And sure, everyone does that to some extent — catches signals behind what's been said by the tone of voice and expression on the person's face and all that. But this was different.

It was like everything was sharper and clearer — as though I was looking at the world with magnified sight and hearing.

This might sound nuts but I swear I was starting to pick up things from some of my teachers just from the way they breathed. Like when Madame Ploudier takes attendance in French class. She calls out names and everyone says, "Ici," when she gets to theirs. Only, I couldn't.

I noticed that by the third day of my silence, when Madame called my name (which she pronounces Gree-FEN, with the emphasis on "fen") her voice got a tired, kind of impatient sound to it. And, of course, since I couldn't answer, she had to glance over at my desk to see if I was there.

You wouldn't think that would be much of a big deal, but trust me, I could feel her tension level rising every single day. On Friday, by the time she reached the kids whose last names started with M, there was a definite edge to her voice.

So on Monday, I thought maybe I should do something — before she got fed up enough to blow. Anytime that happens she yells and stomps, waving her arms and just generally freaking out. I could live with that — it's actually kind of entertaining — but she always wraps up the performance by doubling our assignments for about a week.

Trust me, you don't want to be the kid in Madame's class who sets her off. Now, I couldn't tell if anyone else had noticed how aggravated she was getting over my silence, but there was no point in taking a chance.

So, by the time I got to class on Monday, I was prepared. When I went in, I went straight to Madame's desk and passed her a note that said, "Madame Ploudier, je suis ici aujourd'hui." I'd added my name and the date underneath.

Madame picked the note up and read it. For a second or two she looked puzzled, and maybe a little angry, but then her expression softened. I watched to see what would happen when she took attendance and to my relief there were no signs that she was getting steamed as she got close to me. When she got to my name she tapped the note and just continued on to the next person.

That was one problem solved, but it was obvious there were going to be others. With the speeches still a week away from even starting (and it would take a good week for everyone to have had a turn) I really wanted to avoid complications with teachers if I could.

Unfortunately, it seemed Mr. Durkin had other ideas. Now, since he's a Math teacher (and you really don't need to talk all that much in Math class), that might seem odd. But not if you know Mr. Durkin.

The first thing you'd think if you ever met him would be that he had to be *way* past retirement age. He walks with a cane and dresses in old cardigans and grey pants with baggy knees, and his hair looks like it was styled by Albert Einstein's barber.

However old he really is, he's still teaching at West-ingford Middle School. And even though he shuffles around and looks like he's in the advanced stages of senility, there are plenty of kids who could tell you what a mistake it is to let that fool you.

Corey Strickland and Will Pickett learned the hard way at the start of the school year. They always pick seats across from each other and as close as possible to the back of the room. Of course, that's only until the teach-ers separate them and move them to the front, which never takes long.

Anyway, Corey and Will took one look at Mr. Durkin on the first day of school in September, and thought they had it made. Not only did they figure there was nothing to worry about as far as the usual seating rearrangements were concerned, they also saw the opportunity to have a little fun with the old boy.

It started on Wednesday of the second week, when Durkin was checking attendance.

"Pickett, William," he called, his voice raspy and thin.

"Here," said Corey.

And, of course, when he called out Corey's name, Will answered. Durkin never batted an eye, but then, how many teachers could have gotten their students all figured out that fast? With four classes, that's a hundred faces and names to remember in a few days.

The next day the guys went back to being themselves, but on Friday they switched again.

On Monday everyone knew they'd be pretending to be each other again. Only, it didn't happen, because when Durkin got to the P's, he switched things around and called out, "Pickett, Corey," instead of "Pickett, William."

Corey (who was supposed to answer as Will) was too confused to say anything. Same for Will when Durkin asked for, "Strickland, William."

"Ah, it's Corey, sir," Corey said after a few seconds. "Corey Strickland."

"And is that you, young man?" Durkin asked peering at him.

"Yes, sir."

"And you, young Pickett," he turned to Will. "What, pray tell, is your first name?"

"Will, sir."

"I see." Durkin looked back and forth between them for a long, silent moment. "Then perhaps the two of you can explain your recent confusion over your identities."

Neither had anything to say.

"You *do* have an explanation, I assume," Durkin continued. "Because if you don't, that would mean your intention was to make a fool of me." He paused. "*Was* that your intention? To make *me* look foolish?"

"No, sir," they said at once.

"I thought not." Durkin looked at them steadily. It wasn't a mean or threatening look, but there was something unnerving in his expression just the same. I was sitting pretty close to the back of the class and I can tell you, everyone was holding their breath and there was a lot of tension in the room. None of us knew what to expect, but we were suddenly wide awake to the fact that this was no doddering old fool in front of us.

Then he smiled and his whole face brightened, like he'd just had an idea. Except, the idea hadn't just occurred to him then and there, that was for sure, because he reached into the desk, pulled out a couple of flat, triangular things, and opened them to reveal cone-shaped hats. They were pink with big purple dots.

"Perhaps this will help end the confusion," Durkin said, nodding encouragingly to Will and Corey. He turned the hats and we could see that he'd printed their names on them with gold glitter. "Come get them, boys."

Will and Corey made their way to the front and took the hats. They started back to their seats, holding the ugly things in their hands.

"On your heads, boys!" Durkin insisted. "This way, if either of you forget who you are again, you need but check the other's hat first. That will tell you who you're *not*, and should therefore, by the process of elimination, be of great assistance to you."

Will and Corey wore those hats in Durkin's class for the next three weeks and I don't suppose I have to tell you they looked like morons in them.

That was just the first of many times we got to see how sharp Durkin really was, in spite of his appearance.

He misses nothing.

I'd known, from the minute I started the whole silence thing, that if anyone would be able to see through it, it would be Durkin. And now, it seemed he was watching me.

Class was almost over, and I was about to breathe a sigh of relief, when he confirmed what I'd been worrying about.

Chapter Fifteen

"Mr. Maxwell," Durkin said, just seconds before the bell rang to end class. "I wonder if I could trouble you for a few moments of your time after school today."

He wonders. Right. Like I had the option of refusing. I nodded and tried to look like the thought didn't send something cold right through my body. I'd thought I was in the clear — nearly two weeks had gone by without him showing any sign of being suspicious. But now, there he was, smiling and looking innocent, the way he always does when he's about to swoop down and strike. The worst thing was, there was no way to prepare myself. Even if I could speak I knew I couldn't outthink or outmanoeuvre him.

Since Math is my second period of the morning, I had the rest of the day to worry about it. I made the most of the opportunity. As I concentrated on thinking up all the dire possibilities, I realized that my biggest problem was the fact that my voice was gone. If Durkin could prove somehow that I wasn't one hundred percent genuine about the soldiers, it was pretty much guaranteed that he'd insist I start talking.

Only, I couldn't!

I'd been trying, believe me. By the old abandoned township hall, near the rock quarry, in the shower — anywhere I could be sure no one was listening. Not that it mattered, since I hadn't been able to get out a single syllable.

I'd tried yelling, thinking I might be able to force something out. Nothing. I'd even tried whispering, but all I'd managed was a cross between a huff and a whistle.

So, if Durkin came down hard on me and expected me to knock off the act and answer him, I was in serious trouble.

By lunchtime I was knotted up inside, and I knew I wasn't going to be able to eat my sandwich or any of the other stuff Mom had packed for me. I took a couple of sips of apple juice and felt my stomach lurch and protest.

Bryan noticed that I wasn't eating and his hand shot out in an offer to take care of my big, chewy oatmeal cookies. I passed them over but couldn't help thinking he could have been a bit more sympathetic.

"Mmm!" he said. He chewed blissfully, eyes closed. "I should get the recipe for these from your mom."

Bryan's mother cooks but she doesn't bake much so

he's learned how to make a few things himself. There's nothing wrong with that, but I don't know why he doesn't keep it a bit quieter. (He even says he's going to take Culinary Industry in high school, but I don't think he'll really do it.)

There were other things on my mind at the moment, though, so I ignored the way he was going on with the cookies, scribbled a note, and passed it to him.

"Durkin, huh?" he said as he read. "That could be trouble." He read on. "So you still can't talk at all, huh?"

I shook my head and waited. Bryan has always been able to come up with good ideas and I was counting on him now.

"I dunno, Griff," he said after a pause, during which he finished off the second cookie. "But really, how solid could he have you, anyway? It's not like he can prove anything, even if he suspects this whole thing is a scam."

I wasn't thrilled with the word "scam."

"So ... I guess the best thing for you to do is stand your ground if he confronts you. Maybe that would even convince him he's wrong. In any case, it's not like you have a lot of options, since you can't talk anyway."

Compared to some of the schemes he's come up with, this didn't sound like much of a plan to me, but then he hadn't had a whole lot of time either. I tried not to look worried.

"Griffin?"

I turned to see Linda Granville standing behind me. She smiled and looked at me expectantly, like she was waiting for me to acknowledge her.

"You do know he can't talk, don't you?" Bryan said.

"Oh, yeah! I forgot!" She giggled like that was hilarious, hand over her mouth and shoulders kind of hunched.

"So, anyway, what I wanted," she said when she'd gotten control of herself, "was to ask you a question. Actually, more than one, but that would be later."

It looked for a second as though she was going to take another laughing fit, but she pulled herself together and went on. "I guess you know that I'm a reporter with the school paper. Well, I've been the editor too, but we take turns with that so it's someone else this time.

"And what I was wondering was, if it would be possible to interview you for the next edition. About you not talking and stuff. Of course it would have to be done in writing," she added quickly, to show that she'd thought it all through. "I figured I'd ask questions and you could write down the answers. Like that."

"Yeah, well, he's not interested," Bryan said, accurately reading the look on my face.

"Why *not*?" Linda looked right at me. "I mean, if you care so much about this cause I'd think you'd be happy for a chance to get the information about it out there. Otherwise, what's the point of your protest?"

"You're right. He'll do it."

I jerked my head around to look at Bryan, sure that I'd see some sign that he was joking, but his face was dead serious.

"Okay! Well, that's great then." Linda looked like she might clap her hands. "When can we get started?"

I glowered at Bryan, who cheerfully and deliberately ignored me. Instead, he told Linda that she could get a list of questions together for me and I'd write out the answers for her as soon as I could. They talked over details, like what would be done if she had any questions about what I wrote and stuff, just like I wasn't sitting right there looking more furious with each second that went by.

"So, I'll get those questions to you tomorrow," Linda said, finally turning back to me. If she noticed that I looked less than enthusiastic, she didn't let on.

"He'll be here," Bryan said with a huge smile. But as soon as she started to walk away, he turned to me and lifted his hands, palms forward.

"I had no choice," he said. "It would have looked too suspicious if you'd refused, and you know she'd have talked about that and people would have wondered. Like she said, you're supposed to be doing this to help a cause. Why would you not want the chance to promote it? This will do a lot to get rid of any doubts anyone might have."

I calmed down after a minute and decided he was right. But none of that was going to make any difference with Durkin.

The thought of the upcoming meeting was starting to make me queasy, and by the time school was out for the afternoon, I just wanted to go see him and get it over with, whatever happened.

CHAPTER SIXTEEN

He was writing up problems on the board when I got to his class, so I just stood in the doorway and waited for him to notice me. He did after a moment, and waved me in almost distractedly while he finished up the equation he'd already started.

"So, Griffin, I imagine you're wondering why I asked you to come by this afternoon."

I nodded and tried not to look either nervous or guilty, though I was both. My heart sank at his next words.

"It's about your protest, actually." He perched on the edge of his desk and motioned for me to pull up a chair.

I knew it!

"There's someone I want to introduce you to, so to speak," he said. I looked toward the doorway automatically, but no one was there.

"No, no." He was smiling, but that meant nothing. I'd seen him smile most sincerely when he was on the verge of pouncing.

While I sat there sweating, Durkin reached into the pocket of his shirt. His hand came out with a picture, but before he passed it to me he paused and looked at it solemnly. When he handed it to me, it was with just the smallest shake of his head.

I don't know what I'd been expecting, but this sure wasn't it! The picture was of a little black kid — he looked about six — dressed in a white shirt and khaki shorts. Strong, perfect teeth shone out from the huge smile on his face.

There was nothing identifying in the background to show where the picture had been taken, but I somehow knew right away it wasn't anywhere in North America.

"This is Kato Musamba," Durkin said quietly. "He was nine three years ago when that shot was taken — a very bright boy. The picture you're holding is my favourite one of him. If you look, you can see the spark in his eyes.

"I was Kato's sponsor — had been since he was seven. I'm sure you're familiar with how that works. There are a number of different organizations — you've heard of them?"

I nodded to show that I knew what he was talking about.

"Kato is from Uganda. Unfortunately, Uganda is one of the African countries where children can be seized and forced into war."

Then, of course, I knew what he was going to say.

Only, I didn't want to hear it. I wanted to give him back the little kid's picture and get out of there. But I couldn't stop him and, of course, he kept going with his story.

"Last year I received word from the sponsorship organization that my sponsorship for Kato had ended and that I was receiving a new child. It took a while for me to find out what had happened to him. Officially, all I was told was that Kato had stopped participating in the program, and no longer qualified for that reason. But I knew something was dreadfully wrong. I knew because of these."

Durkin reached beside him and lifted a large envelope, from which he drew out a thin stack of papers.

"These are Kato's letters. He wrote very faithfully and was clearly an exceptionally gifted child — intelligent, full of life, full of hopes and plans."

Durkin stopped speaking for a few seconds. He cleared his throat before continuing.

"I've photocopied his letters for you. I thought you might be interested in reading them." He slid the pages back into the envelope and passed it to me.

"I'm sure you've guessed by now what really happened to Kato." A heavy breath, slowly expelled. "It took some time and money, but I was able to learn the truth: Kato was captured and forced into combat more than a year ago, when he was only eleven years old."

I looked at him questioningly. Durkin nodded, understanding.

"I was able to find out that he was still alive about three months after he'd been taken, but nothing since then. Unfortunately, even if he survives, it would be foolhardy to think he could emerge from the experience unchanged. *If* he is alive, I fear he is no longer the same boy who posed with this hopeful smile, or wrote these letters."

I stood. I no longer felt anxious to leave but it seemed Durkin was through. There was a peculiar heaviness in my chest that made it hard to breathe.

"Oh, the picture. I'll keep that," he said, reaching for the photo that I still held, "but I've made you a copy of it as well. It's in with the letters.

"Just before you go, Griffin ...," Durkin put a hand on my shoulder, "there's one more thing I wanted to say."

He took another deep breath and looked me square in the eye. "I wanted to say thank you for what you're doing. It's a remarkable thing for a boy your age. So, for Kato and thousands upon thousands of other young boys — and girls — thank you from the bottom of my heart."

I saw, through a blur, that Durkin's hand was extended and I had no choice but to reach out my own for the handshake he was offering.

Inside, I burned with shame.

CHAPTER SEVENTEEN

"Liar."

I was halfway home when I realized I'd spoken out loud. The sound of my voice hung in the air, surprising me almost as much as the word stung.

I glanced around, but there was no one nearby. I put my hand over my mouth, as though I was coughing, and tested to see if I could repeat it.

"Liar."

My first feeling, I might as well admit, was relief. Knowing I could talk again, having my voice back — it lifted a big worry from me. But that was short-lived.

I glanced down at the envelope I was carrying along with my Science book — the one that held copies of Kato's letters and picture. Just a plain old envelope, but every time I looked at it I felt like it was accusing me of something. I moved it so it was behind my notebook.

"Yo! Griffin! Wait up, man!"

I turned and was surprised to see Bryan hurrying up

behind me. I wondered how I'd gotten ahead of him, since I'd stayed behind after school. Maybe he'd gone to the library or something.

"So, what was up with Durkin? Is he on to you?" he asked as he fell in beside me.

I shook my head.

"Excellent! So, what did he want?" He looked over at me expectantly, then shook his head and laughed.

"Sorry, dude. I don't know how I forgot."

I almost opened my mouth to tell him I could talk again, but something held me back. Instead, I gave a "what can you do?" shrug and kept walking.

"Well, it's good that he didn't call you on the protest," Bryan said. "'Cause for sure he'd have gone to the other teachers and then the whole thing would have been for nothing. I hate to see my brilliant plans fall apart."

A flash of anger ran through me. Like that was fair. If I was going to be mad at anyone, it might as well be the person who really deserved it. Me. Everything Bryan had done was to help me out.

By then we'd reached the corner where we take off in different directions. I gave Bryan a quick wave in answer to his, "See ya," and was home in a couple of minutes.

I decided I might as well get right to the envelope Durkin had given me and get it over with, so I started for my room. But before I'd taken two steps, yelling stopped me in my tracks.

"It's not fair! *I'm* never allowed to do anything," Kellie was wailing. "How come Griffin can do whatever he wants and no one says anything, but if *I* want something, oh, that's another story, isn't it?"

"You can carry on as long as you like but you're *not* going to an out-of-town concert in a car driven by some teenaged boy. Period."

Mom wasn't quite yelling back, but she was close to it.

"Yeah, I bet if Griffin asked you'd let *him* go. You let him do everything."

I wondered how I'd gotten dragged into the argument, especially when I didn't even know what they were talking about.

Kellie then went on to describe what a fantastically great and safe driver this kid was and how he'd already had his licence for seven whole months and had never had a single accident. It might have been more convincing if she'd used the dude's real name — if she even knew it — instead of his unfortunate nickname, which happened to be Snake. On the other hand, it might not have made the slightest difference.

As I stood there, not wanting to get any closer to Mom and Kellie while this was going on, the door flew open behind me and Leah stomped in. She slammed the door behind her and tromped down the hall like I wasn't even there.

"Mommy!" she yelled when she was about halfway to the kitchen, "can you phone Rachel's mother and tell her she should ground Rachel?"

"Don't be so mental," Kellie yelled back at her before Mom could even say anything. "Anyway, get out of here. I'm trying to talk to Mom."

"I'm allowed talking to Mommy too!"

"Well, *I'm* talking about something *important*, so you can just wait."

Right about now, Leah should start to cry, I thought, and sure enough she burst out blatting.

"I *can too* talk!" she blubbered.

It went back and forth like this for a few more minutes and then Mom managed to shout "Enough!" over the two of them. In the meantime, Nicole had come down from her room and was heading for the kitchen.

"It's no wonder I don't bring my friends here," she said. "If people in this house aren't screaming, they're not talking at all. It's like living in an insane asylum."

"Like you have friends," Kellie mumbled. That would have started a fresh war, but Mom cut it off before it could get going by telling all three of them to go to their rooms.

Nicole protested that she'd *been* in her room trying to study in the first place. Kellie pointed out that she wasn't finished "discussing" the concert. Leah kept bawling.

Mom told Nicole it worked out well for her then, since she wanted to be in her room anyway. She told Kellie they were most certainly finished talking and one more word would not only mean that she wasn't going to the concert, but that she wouldn't be going anywhere for the next week.

"Here! Wipe your nose, take off your shoes, and go pick up your toys," she said to Leah, cutting her off before she had a chance to repeat Rachel's transgressions.

"And I'd better not hear a single word of arguing from any of you," she cautioned as they filed out into the hallway, where I was still standing. I tried to look like I hadn't heard anything, which didn't save me from the glares I got from Nicole and Kellie as they walked by and clomped up the stairs to their rooms, which are both on the second floor.

Leah emerged last, sniffling and looking forlorn.

"Griffin, can you help me clean up my room?" she asked pitifully, her words coming a couple at a time between shuddering gulps of air.

I nodded and patted her head, feeling suddenly really sorry for her. The poor kid can't begin to stand up for herself around here, not with the psycho sisters around. I don't think I ever noticed before how Leah never seems to get to talk. Even if what she's saying is silly, she should be heard — at least some of the time.

Her room is on the main level like mine and I followed her down the hall and helped her start picking up her stuff. After she got calmed down she told me about the terrible things her friend Rachel had done — not sharing her doll's hair curlers and always "being the big boss of everything" and a few other equally serious offences.

Since I still wasn't officially talking, I just listened and nodded, which seemed to be all she really wanted. In the end, she declared that she *might* give Rachel one more chance before deciding if they were ever, *ever* going to be friends again.

When we'd finished putting her toys in the chest, Leah gave me a kind of shy smile and said thanks.

Then I finally headed to my room to face the stuff Durkin had given me.

CHAPTER EIGHTEEN

I slid the pages out of the envelope and thumbed through them quickly. Durkin had arranged them with Kato's picture on top, followed by the letters, which were in order.

I looked at the photo for a couple of minutes, until it started to bother me. I mean, it was a nice, happy looking picture and everything, but from what Durkin had told me, the kid probably didn't have much to smile about anymore. And a kid is all he was. A little kid at that.

I picked up the top sheet of the letter pages and started to read.

Dear Mr. James Durkin,

My name is Kato Musamba and I am seven years old. Also, I am a boy. I write to you today for the first time with great thanks in my heart for your help to me and my family. I promise that I will study hard in school and learn much.

I hope I will have letter from you before long.
With wishes for your health and happiness,
Kato

Dear Mr. James Durkin,

My heart is full of excitement to receive your letter! When Teacher called my name today I thought I would burst with pride. It is my first time to receive a letter! So, now I will answer your two questions.

The colours that I like best are red in early morning when the sky is on fire and the greens of all growing things. Here in Uganda are many beautiful trees and plants and flowers, for we have much rain for many months of the year.

I have two sisters who are called Sudati and Nagesa and a brother who is called Paskar. I am oldest of all. I am happy to learn of your wife and daughter and grandchildren.

With wishes of health and happiness to you and your family.

Kato

Dear James Durkin,

With much joy I received your letter today! I am very well and happy. I hope you too. In school this morning we studied Social Studies and English and this later day we will study Mathematics. I like Mathematics and Social Studies best. Teacher says I learn quickly. Then I feel satisfied that I will be a good student. Father says that if I study hard someday maybe I will work in a big building in the city. Maybe even Kampala. That is our country's capital.

My favourite sport is soccer. We play with a ball made from cloth. I am not so fast as the bigger boys but my friend Akello can play very well. He runs like a cheetah but I run like a monkey. Even though I am not a best player, it is great fun. Do you like soccer?

> With fond wishes for all good to you,
> Kato

Dear James Durkin,

I am joyful to receive your letter today. I am very well and happy. I hope you too. I like the pictures you sent of you and your family. I showed my classmates the pictures and their eyes were very surprised to see the snow. Teacher told us snow is same like ice but not so hard. Once, when I was smaller, my family had to go to Entebbe and when we were there I had water with a piece of ice in it. I could not stop touching it! How cold and slippery it was. I would like to see this snow someday. Are you having it every year?

We are having dry season. Those days are so hot, to 35 degrees. In rainy season it is cooler, to 27 degrees. Each night we walk to town for sleeping and I like dry season best for this. In rainy times our mats are wet and it is more difficult to sleep.

> With great affection,
> Kato

The next few pages of letters were a lot like these — mostly the kinds of things you might talk about to anyone you're getting to know, except for the fact that Kato's life was so different from anything we'd ever experience. I could see why Durkin cared so much about this kid. There was definitely something about him that made you like him right away.

I was curious as to what he meant about walking to town to sleep, though, because I knew from other things he'd said that he lived in a small village. I thought I remembered something about it in one of the articles I'd read, so I put down the letters and thumbed through the printouts.

I found information on it after a few minutes and wondered why it hadn't sunk in before. About 35,000 kids have to leave their homes *every evening* and walk for miles and miles to towns in order to keep from being kidnapped by the Lord's Resistance Army — or LRA.

I kept reading, and found out that more than 20,000 Ugandan children had been captured by the LRA over the years, and that making these nightly treks was how the children in northern parts of the country protected themselves. I couldn't picture leaving my house every night, walking for, say, five miles, and then sleeping on a mat outside a school or hospital or some other place.

For the kids who had been kidnapped by the LRA, some of the most horrible things you can imagine had happened. As sickening as it was, I forced myself to read more articles about kids who were forced to kill other kids, or their own family members, just to stay alive. That was kind of like their introduction into the army, which is headed by a tyrant named Joseph Kony. No wonder they walk to places they hope will be safe night after night. And this has been going on for a lot of them since they were old enough to walk in the first place.

It was amazing how cheerful and optimistic Kato managed to be in spite of the terrible circumstances he had to live with. He wrote cheerful bits of information about his life as if everything was normal.

Well, it was normal for him, I guess. You wouldn't believe what they eat over there! I can tell you I wasn't too impressed. No pizza or burgers or fries, for one thing. He talked about stuff like cassava, maize, beans, and rice like they were delicious. I looked up some of the foods he mentioned just so I could have some idea what he was talking about. There was something called sorghum porridge with lemon juice or sour milk and sugar. Sounds pretty gross, huh? Or matoke — which is mashed, steamed bananas, though why you'd want to do that to bananas instead of just eating them normal I have no idea.

Once in a while Kato mentioned having fish, or chicken or beef, which seemed to be a treat to him, so I guess they didn't have those things too often.

Other things that seemed to be his favourites — such as bean cakes (mashed black beans with some vegetables,

rolled in flour and fried) or peanut soup (where the pea-
nuts are ground and then cooked with water and milk)
— didn't sound too appealing either. He even talked
about eating grasshoppers. I thought maybe he was
joking but I found out it's true — they eat them, and
white ants, too. Gross!!

I guess it's what you're used to. Maybe their diet
is even healthier than ours in some ways. I gotta tell
you, though, I'd just as soon take my chances with
fast foods.

But it wasn't just the stuff they ate that made Kato's
life so different from anything I could begin to imagine.
His village had no running water. No indoor bathrooms
or showers. And they had to go to a well and carry home
all the water they needed.

And no electricity! I stopped reading for a few minutes and tried to think of all the times and ways my family
uses electricity in a single day. You should try it — you'll
be amazed. Just in the kitchen alone there's the fridge,
stove, dishwasher, toaster, microwave, mixer, grill, coffee
pot, blender, can opener ... and we don't have half the
gadgets at our place that some people have!

Durkin must have checked out a few things because
he'd made a couple of notes in the margin. For example,
the average income for families like Kato's was only *four
to six dollars a week.*

The thing that struck me the most was how much
that kid loved school! Not just because he was willing

to make that long walk twice a day, but because of the way he talked about it. He got so excited about some of the stuff he learned. If anyone at my school acted that enthusiastic about learning, well, I don't have to tell you what everyone would think of them. Funny thing was, it didn't seem strange to read about it from Kato. Like, in this letter:

Dear James D.

Your letter, most welcome as always, comes on a special day! Today we have received new books for our classroom. Teacher let us come to the front to see them and my heart beat so strong when it was my turn. We are too many, so we cannot all go at once.

When I looked at the books, four big books with many things for us to learn, I almost cannot swallow because of excitement! They are bright colours, and we can smell the newness of the paper. But we may only look on the outside, even though I know there are pictures inside. It is very hard not to open!

Someday, I will work in large building in city and I will buy a book, maybe more than one! Then I will open it at any time I want.

I study very hard every day and Teacher says I am a best student. But other days he says I am like a naughty chimpanzee. So I must try to improve always.

Your students are lucky to have you for so few. In my class we are 93 students and one Teacher.

*I am happy to hear news of your family that everyone is
well and you too.*

I send you many hugs.

> *With much love,*
>
> *Kato*

I sat the pages down then, and picked up his picture.
I thought about how Durkin had shook my hand. I
thought about how I'd used horrible things that happened to kids like Kato just to get out of an assignment.
After a minute I felt something wet on my face.

"I'm sorry," I whispered, and I meant it. Then I took
a deep breath.

"I, Griffin John Maxwell ..."

I took the vow. Only this time, I honestly meant it.

CHAPTER NINETEEN

Bryan looked up at me from across the table in the cafeteria, his face puzzled.

"What do you mean, it's real now?" he asked. The note I'd given him apparently hadn't been clear enough.

I did my best to explain it more, writing down details of some of horrible things being done to kids — a lot of them younger than us. I ended with some stuff about Kato.

Bryan took his time and read it all. Watching his eyes, I saw him finish and then reread it from the start. Then he put the page down and looked across the table at me. For a minute, he said nothing. Then he nodded, real slow and serious.

"Cool." He paused long enough to bite a chunk off his sandwich, chew and swallow. "So, what were you planning to do?"

Do? Even though my folks had been asking me that question more and more often, I hadn't actually given it much thought. Since the whole thing had been bogus, I hadn't seen the need to figure out any kind of plan. But now, it was embarrassingly obvious that just being silent for however long wasn't going to be particularly useful.

What *could* I do that would help kids who were so far away?

I scribbled down the admission that I hadn't actually figured that out and then added the one-word question, "Ideas?"

"Well," he said, "there'd be the obvious things, like contacting the local paper to see if they'd do a story about it. Sending the story in to the radio station. Seeing if storeowners in the area would get involved. That kind of thing."

None of that had been obvious to me, but I didn't bother trying to let him know that. I was too busy thinking about how awful it would be to have all that attention focused on me. I mean, I was the guy who'd started this whole thing because I didn't want to talk in front of a couple dozen kids.

"What you really need," Bryan added, "is a *tangible* goal."

I probably looked as lost as I felt because he jumped into an explanation right away.

"Like, a specific thing you want to accomplish. For example, if you wanted to raise X number of dollars, or get a certain number of people to sign up for something, or whatever. As long as it's something measurable.

That's the main thing."

"How come?" I wrote.

"Because otherwise, how will you know when to start talking again? You'll still be going around like a mime — and not a very good one, I might add — twenty years from now. You *do* realize that you're not going to be able to do anything that will actually put an end to kids fighting in wars, don't you?"

I thought about that for a minute. Not to sound like an idiot — I did know that one person couldn't stop what was happening — but I wanted to do something that would really matter somehow. Bryan's ideas were good, but I didn't see much coming of them.

I wrote: "Let me think about it," and slid the paper to him.

"Sure," he said. "In the meantime, you've got that interview with Linda Granville. It will be good practice for the real paper. In fact, how about if we put together a press release for the *Westingford News* and the radio station? That will answer most of their questions up front. Then they'll probably just want to ask you a few things, like how'd you get interested in this whole thing in the first place."

I must have looked horrified when he said that, because he quickly added, "You're not going to tell the truth about that, of course. Just stick with the original story."

I was distracted from having to think about that by a swat across the top of my head. Startled, I looked up to see Bo Werner hovering over me like some kind of freak in a horror movie.

"Hey, Do-gooder," he smirked. "I need some, uh, assistance with my History. Seems I got behind a bit in my notes."

He tossed his notebook on the table in front of me.

"Take your time, though. I don't need it 'til tomorrow." He laughed good and loud at that. Quite the wit, that Bo. "And it better be done right, unless you want another round of that butt-kicking I gave you."

I sat perfectly still.

"Now, take good care of that there notebook, little buddy," he said giving me a slap on the back that almost sent me sprawling forward.

He walked away while I stared at the notebook. It was in pretty pathetic shape. The cover pages were torn and curled, not to mention scribbled all over.

Glancing up, I saw that Bryan was looking at it too. After a minute he picked it up and flipped to the last used page.

"Hasn't been touched for over two weeks," he said. "And we've had a lot of homework in History lately. It will take you the whole evening to do this."

That answered it for me. I shook my head.

"You're *not* going to do it?" Bryan asked. I shook my head again, which prompted him to ask about the state of my sanity.

I shrugged. Going by Bryan's expression, which was

half shocked and half impressed, I'm guessing that I looked a lot braver than I felt.

The truth was, I wasn't going to do Bo's homework for the simple reason that I didn't have time. My essay was due the next day, and after the way everything had hit me last night, there were a lot of things I wanted to change in what I'd written. In fact, I might have to do the whole thing over. Anyway, considering the subject I was writing about, a few knuckles in the face just didn't seem like that big of a deal.

I'd gotten through it before, I guessed I could do it again.

So, when I walked out of the cafeteria to head to afternoon classes, I left Bo's notebook sitting right where it was on the table.

CHAPTER TWENTY

Linda caught me in the hallway between English and Science.

"Griffin, there you are!" She looked pretty flustered as she dug through her stuff and finally pulled out a sheet of paper. "I've got that list of questions for you."

She thrust the page at me like it was a live grenade and added, "The next edition of the school paper comes out a week from Thursday, so if you could have your answers to me by Friday, then we can go over anything I need to ask — maybe sometime on the weekend if that's all right with you. I've already reserved the front page and a whole page inside — probably page two or three — so include as much detail as you can, okay?"

I nodded.

"Great. So, that's giving you enough time? Well, I guess you won't know until you start working on it. But if it's not, just let me know and maybe you could finish on the weekend and I could come by and we could wrap the whole thing up at once. If that's convenient for you, I mean."

The way she was babbling on and on struck me as really comical after a few minutes, but her face was so earnest that it would have been mean to laugh. I just kept nodding and finally she seemed to run out of things to say. Or, maybe it was because she could see we were both going to be late for our next classes.

I took her questions home with me and actually found some of them helpful when I was working on the essay. The new essay, that is. I didn't have time to start writing out answers for her, but then it occurred to me that I could probably just give her a copy of my essay. I'd only have to write out the answers to anything that wasn't covered in there.

I was so engrossed in the whole thing that I even forgot about Bo and his threat. Until I got to school the next morning, that is.

To say Bo didn't look happy when it started to sink into his caveman head that not only had I not done his homework, I didn't even have his notebook, would be something of an understatement. He was in such a rage that he actually looked like he might have gone over the edge.

"*Where's* my book?" he yelled for the third time, as if I hadn't made it good and clear that I didn't have it.

"What's the problem, boys?"

We turned at the same time (though I doubt Bo felt

the relief I did) to see Mr. Morris, the principal, standing a few feet away.

"This little weasel stole my History notebook," Bo claimed. He looked so indignant that it actually seemed believable. Luckily, Morris knew his reputation.

"Uh huh. And why would he do that?"

"I loaned it to him for ... see ... he wanted to check something."

"What?"

"Whadyamean?"

"I mean, what did he want to check?"

"I dunno. He just said he needed it." Bo, clearly under the impression that Morris was actually buying his story, went a bit overboard. "I didn't ask no questions, I just gave it to him. That's the kinda guy I am. I like, uh, helping people."

Morris took a deep, slow breath and turned to me. "Did you borrow his book?" he asked, in the tone of voice you use when you're just going through the motions of something.

I shook my head.

"I guess that's clear," he said, addressing Bo again. "Griffin doesn't have your book."

"You don't know that," Bo said. I could see he was trying hard to hold onto his temper, but judging by the way his face was turning red he was going to lose it any minute.

"In fact, I do."

126

"Just 'cause the little weasel says so ..."

"Actually, it's because your book is in the office."

This news took Bo by surprise. He opened his mouth but couldn't seem to find anything to say.

"It was turned in yesterday after lunch. Apparently, it was left on a table in the cafeteria."

"He musta left it there!" Bo said, like that proved everything.

"Well, that's not what I heard. And I've been hearing some pretty interesting things in the past few days. So, this little hallway spat was rather fortuitous, because I meant to speak to you two gentlemen today, anyway."

Once again Bo was rendered speechless. Then Morris told us to come with him to the office. Bo tried to worm out of it.

"I, uh, can't miss my first class," he sputtered. "We're doing something real important today."

"*Really?* What's the subject?" Morris asked him.

I can't even describe how dumb Bo looked when he couldn't answer that. Morris just stood there for a minute, watching him strain his brain in the effort to actually think. The second time Morris told us to come with him, Bo didn't argue.

Once we were in his office, Morris laid it all out. Apparently, someone had filled him in on the whole story of Bo beating up on me. And they'd told him about the current threat over the History work.

"Ain't true, none of it," Bo said.

"Griffin?" Morris asked.

I sat stone-faced and refused to give any indication one way or the other. I didn't like the idea of getting knocked around again, but it was still better than being a rat.

Morris sat and looked at both of us for a few minutes. Seemed that if I didn't back up what he'd heard, he was going to have to drop the whole thing. But he didn't. I guess he understood how it was, because he spoke up again after a bit.

"Well, sometimes rumours turn out to be false," he said. "On the other hand, sometimes they turn out to be true. I guess the only way we'll know about this particular matter is if, in fact, Griffin shows up at school with any evidence of having been in a fight. Especially a fight with someone who is clearly bigger and stronger than him, although I prefer not to think that Bo is the kind of coward who would stoop that low.

"However, if there is a fight, there *will* be a thorough investigation. And if I have to ask every student at this school about it, I *will* have the truth.

"And just so I'm perfectly, crystal clear, Mr. Werner — if I learn that there has been any, and I do mean any, aggression on your part toward *any* student, you will be facing a permanent expulsion."

He paused, cleared his throat, and added. "I'll be contacting your mother and advising her of the situation as well. We would all like to see you get an education and become a productive member of society, but this school will not tolerate bullying or violence."

Bo actually looked alarmed at the mention of his mother. Mostly, though, he looked like he'd just been cheated of something.

And me? I guess I felt relieved.

CHAPTER TWENTY-ONE

I handed my essay in that Friday morning and at lunchtime I gave Linda a copy of it, along with the answers I'd written to questions that the essay didn't cover. Well, there was one that I just left out, hoping she wouldn't notice with all the other information she had. That question was: How did you first become interested in the plight of child soldiers?

I didn't want to lie anymore, but I wasn't keen to tell the truth either. I'd decided that if I was really cornered with that kind of question, I'd just say it was private. I hoped that would work if Linda or anyone else pushed for an answer.

I had also requested a meeting with Durkin after school and was really hoping he'd be able to help me out. The plan Bryan had come up with earlier in the week about having a specific goal seemed like a good idea, only I hadn't been able to figure out exactly what the best kind of goal would be. Really, what could I do that would make a difference to kids who'd been seized from their homes, and were being forced to fight and kill?

Bryan had pointed out that without a specific goal, I could be stuck not talking for who knows how long. I needed something to shoot for so I'd know when it was done.

That had actually got me thinking, what do I really need to talk for? Would it matter that much if I didn't talk for a year? Five years? How much had I ever said that was worth anything?

Besides, like I mentioned before, something interesting had been happening in the few short weeks I'd been silent. I was starting to like the way I could see and hear things that I'd never noticed before.

I know they say that if you lose a sense, the rest of them try to make up for it by becoming sharper. Well, I think this was something like that. It was as if shutting down my own voice had enabled me to really hear other people.

Not that they seemed louder or anything like that. But they were coming through better. I was starting to really "get" what other people meant, and that wasn't all just because of what they said.

I don't know if I'm explaining this right, and I want to. See, when you're not talking, or busy thinking about what you're going to say, you just automatically pay more attention to what's going on around you.

Like, I'd catch it if someone smiled but it wasn't a real smile. And I was understanding what different tones or expressions or movements meant a lot better than I ever had before.

For example at my place the other day, I was watching a show on TV with the girls and Kellie asked Nicole about a top. Seemed Kellie wanted to borrow it but Nicole said no. Only that wasn't the end of it.

"You'll stretch it," she said.

"You are *such* a maggot," Kellie said.

I probably don't need to tell you that it didn't stop there, but that's not my point. See, Kellie normally would have whined or bugged her about the top for a while and then just dropped it. All Nicole had to say was "no." She didn't have to say, "you'll stretch it."

It's not even *like* Nicole to be mean on purpose, so it didn't make sense — her saying that — unless you saw the look in her eyes. Clear as anything, they said she was totally fed-up. Can't really blame her either, considering the way Kellie goes on all the time, being bossy and saying mean things to everyone, and just generally being a huge pain.

The really surprising thing came from Kellie, though. Not that she called Nicole a maggot — that was just normal talk for Kellie. It was how she said it. Normally, I'd have registered the words (if I didn't have them completely tuned out) and that would have been it. But this time I noticed other stuff and it kind of shocked me.

Kellie's shoulders sagged for a second, and then she pushed them up, squaring them off. She shoved her chin out the same way, and you'd think she was being all angry and defiant. But there was something else on her face for a second: a shadow that flashed just long enough to be seen if you were paying attention.

I can hardly describe the look, but I knew right away what it meant. Kellie got all defensive and nasty because she believed what Nicole said was true. And I realized that Kellie goes around acting like she's better than everybody else to cover up the truth — she doesn't think she's as good!

I felt sorry, then, that Nicole had said that mean thing, even though you couldn't really blame her.

And that's just one small example of the things you see and hear when you're not talking. So, like I said, I didn't think it would be a big deal for me not to talk for however long it takes, because it's kind of cool to be seeing all this new stuff.

Maybe even when I am talking again, I can remember how to pay attention — if I can keep from getting distracted by my own voice.

In the meantime, I had to figure out what to do and I was hoping Mr. Durkin would have an idea when I got to his class after school. I'd written out what I wanted earlier, so when I got there I just went in and handed him the note.

He nodded for me to take a seat, and then read the

note. It took a minute because I'd included Bryan's ideas along with a comment at the end saying that while they were good, they weren't quite what I was looking for.

"Naturally," he said when he'd finished, "you *do* need something to work toward. So, the first thing you need to establish is what you hope to accomplish. My guess is that raising public awareness would be it."

I nodded.

"So, you need a secondary goal in order to feel you've achieved your primary goal." He was silent for a few minutes. He rubbed his chin and looked past me toward the back of the room.

"What about a petition, to send to our government asking that the concerns of these citizens be made known in all countries where children are being employed as soldiers?"

A petition! I liked that idea a lot. That would mean people would have to hear about it first — or else how would they know to sign?

I guess I looked excited at the idea, because Durkin smiled and clasped his hands together.

"So, I suppose you'll need a goal of a certain number of signatures. Westingford isn't exactly huge, but I think you could realistically aim for, oh, five hundred."

I picked up the paper and looked around for a pen.

"You don't look too impressed," he said. "How about a thousand, then?"

I found a pen, wrote down a number, and passed him the paper. He looked down.

"A *million* signatures?" he read.

I nodded, happy at the thought. I took the paper and wrote again.

Durkin looked at me with a really big smile after he'd read my final note.

"I think you're right," he said. "You *will* do it!"

Chapter Twenty-Two

"This is great!"

That was Bryan's immediate reaction to the idea of getting a million people to sign a petition, which just goes to show what a good sport he is. Not only was he not one bit put out that I hadn't gone with any of his suggestions, he was instantly one hundred percent behind the new plan.

"So, you have any thoughts on how you're going to get this many signatures?" he asked.

I scribbled quickly and I noticed he looked pleased to see that the first thing I said was we could use his ideas to contact the local media.

"Yeah, sure, but that's not going to get you a million names," he said. I could see he was just thinking out loud at that point; he wasn't looking for my opinion.

"It'll probably just spread and grow on its own," he said after a bit. "Maybe we can even contact some big daily papers and see if they're interested in the story."

So we did that. We sent faxes and Bryan even called a few, but we didn't seem to be attracting any attention. In the meantime, the local paper agreed to do a story, and they did, but it was short, buried near the back of the paper, and while they mentioned the petition they didn't include any clear information about how people could sign it.

The radio station was interested at first, but when they found out they couldn't interview me on the air, they just said they'd be in touch. They weren't.

By the time all of that had happened, we had a total of 137 signatures on the four petition sheets that we were circulating. I'd begun to think I might never get to speak again.

It was, of all people, Mira Travis who came up with the idea of a website. Ever since I quit talking, she'd stopped sending her flaky friends over to give me idiotic messages, and just spoke to me herself. I think it was because it seemed safe to her. As long as I wasn't talking she could just pop by and rave for a few minutes and then take off without worrying that I was going to tell her to get lost. (Which I felt like doing.)

"How's it going, Griffin?" she asked, sliding in across from me at lunch one day. "Never mind, I know you can't answer. But I was wondering: how are you making out with your petition thing? Uh, tap once on the table if it's going good, and twice if it's not."

I figured I might as well answer her, since it was the most likely way of getting rid of her quickly. I tapped twice.

"Huh. Well, I was thinking about that, and I have an idea. You wanna know what it is?"

I shrugged, which most people wouldn't see as much encouragement. Mira, however, is not most people.

"Okay, then. Great! Here it is." To my surprise, she hauled out a detailed plan of reaching people through the internet.

"See, it starts out with the web page, then you have the e-mail campaign, and people all over the country will print out the forms from the site, get one hundred signatures on them, and mail them to you."

I looked the plan over. It was worth thinking about, but it would need a properly designed web page, not something slapped together by an amateur.

Bryan arrived just then and was about to tell Mira we had to talk (the way he usually got rid of her for me if she was there when he came along) but he stopped when I pointed to the page with her plan.

"Looks like a decent idea," he said after he'd looked it over. "Who would do the website?"

"My big brother, Duane," she said. "He knows all about web design and stuff like that. I already asked him and he said he'd do it."

Bryan was looking the plan over for a second time when she dropped the bomb.

"There's just one little thing I'd like in return."

She'd said it in the most innocent tone you can

imagine but the way she smiled at me told me it wasn't going to be as harmless as she'd made it sound.

"If we help you get your million signatures, will you take me to the June dance?"

Westingford Middle School has a dance at the end of the school year but I didn't have the slightest intention of going, least of all with Mira Travis. For one thing, it's a stupid dress-up deal, where instead of wearing something comfortable like jeans, you have to put on a stupid suit or whatever. Plus, I heard that you have to get your date a corsage and there's no way I'm about to start buying flowers for girls.

My automatic reaction was to shake my head "no" — emphatically! But something made me hesitate and that was just enough time for Kato's face to flash through my thoughts. It stopped me from saying "no," but I couldn't bring myself to agree with the plan, either.

Bryan was watching me, trying to read my face to know what I wanted to say. I could see he was confused, which wasn't surprising. I guess it would have been pretty hard to figure out, if what was going on in my head was showing on my face.

"He'll let you know later," he said at last.

She smiled like it was all settled and I was probably going to start checking out corsages on my way home from school, which gave me a bit of a sick feeling.

On the other hand, I knew I probably didn't have much choice. The only question was whether or not I could actually convince myself to go to the dance — and take Mira!

A sinking feeling in my gut told me I wasn't going to have a choice.

CHAPTER TWENTY-THREE

What could I do?

You might be thinking I could very easily have just taken the idea and found someone else to help with it. To be honest, a few weeks ago, I'd probably have done exactly that. But after all that had happened lately, the one thing I thought I'd learned something about was honour. No way was I going to steal Mira's idea and try to convince myself it was okay.

I let Mira know at the end of the day that I would take her to the dance, as long as she understood that did *not* mean we were a couple or dating or anything like that. The deal (I stressed with heavy underlining) was *only* to go to that dance, nothing else. I hoped she realized that meant she'd better not to be expecting me to kiss her.

Bryan had agreed ahead of time that he'd come to Mira's place with me when her brother was building the site and getting all the facts down. I figured it would take an hour or two, but that turned out to be way off.

We worked at it for almost five hours the first time we went there, which was that Saturday afternoon. And that was just a start. Turns out there was a lot more involved in doing a website and getting everything set up than I'd thought.

For one thing, Duane wasn't exactly the web page expert Mira had led us to believe, though he knew more than the rest of us. There was a lot of trial and error, not to mention problems with the whole layout. Eventually he got the main page set up and even though it had taken a while it did look pretty dramatic and interesting.

"So, that's a good start," he said. "We'll finish up next time."

Except next time turned out to be four more times and every one of them lasted at least two or three hours.

I was surprised that Mira didn't hang around and bug me while we were working on all the stuff for the site. A lot of the time she wasn't even in the room we were in, and when she did come in it was usually to bring in snacks and drinks. She did sit in a recliner in the corner and read a few times, but you couldn't say she was an actual nuisance doing that, either.

Once the site was finished it was pretty cool. Duane had found (and got permission to use) some shocking pictures for the main page. They were hard to look at, but they told it like it is, which was our goal.

He'd put a few short paragraphs from my essay right in the middle of the page, with a link for anyone who wanted to read the whole thing. There were also links to some of the big organizations that were fighting to help these kids.

The heading was: "One Voice Silenced: One Million Voices Needed!" There was a short explanation about the protest of silence and the petition, plus a link to a downloadable petition form. My name and mailing address were at the bottom of the form.

Hopefully, anyone who went to the site and read about what was happening to these kids would want to help them. All they had to do was print off the petition form, get a hundred signatures on it, and send it to me.

"So," Duane said when everything was up and running, "your only problem now is getting people to the site. You have any plan for how to do that?"

"We can send out e-mails," Bryan said. "So can our folks. We'll ask them to e-mail the link to friends and family members, and ask those people to do the same. These things spread pretty fast once they get going."

"Yeah, that might work," Duane said.

"You should have something written for them to send," Mira said, looking up from her novel. "Then it can just be forwarded and you don't have to worry about the message getting messed up."

"Good point," Bryan said. "But nothing too long. You ever get one of those messages that would take half an hour to read? Everyone just deletes those."

"A paragraph is enough," Mira agreed. She put her

book down and came over, nudging Duane out of his chair. Plopping herself down, she started to type.

"Okay, is this basically what you're going to want to say?" she asked after a minute. We looked over her shoulder and saw that she'd typed a few important details about the child soldiers and some information about the petition. At the end, she'd just put: "Please, will you help?" followed by the link to the website.

"It's perfect," Bryan said. "Anyone who's going to check out the link will be ready to after reading that, and putting a bunch more stuff wouldn't persuade anyone who isn't interested by that point anyway."

I thought so too, and nodded beside Bryan.

Mira copied what she'd written to a couple of disks and handed them to us.

"So, okay then, I guess this is done," she said. "I'm going to start e-mailing it tonight — to some aunts and uncles and a few friends who might pass it on to their parents."

"This should work," Bryan predicted as we walked toward our places a bit later. "Even if you don't get a whole million names, you'll probably get enough to do some good."

I shook my head to let him know I wasn't going to settle for anything less than the full million signatures.

"You think that's really the right attitude?" he asked. I could see he was either annoyed or maybe disgusted. "I mean, think about it. This thing was totally bogus when it started out, remember? But it's not that way anymore. It matters to you now, and it matters to other people, too."

He didn't say "like me," but he didn't have to. I knew.

"So, my point is, it's not about *you*, Griff, it's about these kids all over the world. And, whatever can be done, however many people sign, it's for *them*. You're not the martyr here."

His words stung. I also thought he was being a bit unfair. After all, I wasn't doing this for myself ... not one bit.

After all, I don't even *like* attention. Remember?

CHAPTER TWENTY-FOUR

Mira showed up at my door four days later, toting some empty boxes. She tried to pass this off as her only reason for coming by, but I wasn't buying it. I know how these things work. An innocent drop-in now, another one later, and the next thing you know she'll be at my place all the time. In fact, if it had been close to a mealtime, Mom would have invited her automatically, and then who knows what kind of crazy ideas she'd get in her head.

And there I was, not even able to object!

"I got my dad to bring these home," she said, holding a box out. A few others were stacked beside her. "They're for packages of paper, which I figured will be just right. I thought you'd need something to store the petitions in when they start coming."

I took the box she was thrusting toward me, grabbed the others and tossed them inside, then gave her a quick thumbs-up, and shut the door as fast as I could. I looked out the peek-hole and saw her standing there looking kind of startled. Maybe a bit hurt, too, but that wasn't my problem. I mean, I hadn't asked her to come.

She turned after a bit of hesitation and walked away, holding her shoulders back and her chin up, like she hadn't just gotten a door slammed in her face.

Okay, I didn't feel that great doing it, but I had to get the message across to her before things got out of hand.

The empty boxes Mira had brought seemed a bit ridiculous. There were four of them, and each one had held a total of 2,500 sheets of paper. It seemed like a lot of space for petition papers.

I stuck them downstairs in the laundry room, just in case I needed one. Or maybe even two of them.

The first few pages came trickling in the next week, and it was kind of exciting, but they'd been mailed locally. I wondered how that had happened so fast until my dad told me he'd taken a few to local stores and merchants had displayed them for customers to sign.

"I'll drop off a few more, since that worked out pretty good," he said. I could see he was pleased that he'd done something to help.

The next week they came in a bit faster. Monday there were two, Tuesday another two, Wednesday seven, Thursday eight, and Friday twenty-two! I put them, along with the few that had come the week before, into the first box. They looked lost in there.

"You got *lots* of tishuns, right, Griffin?" Leah said at dinner on Saturday.

"They're called 'petitions', and he only has a few," Nicole corrected her. She rolled her eyes to show us how impressed she was.

"More than forty, actually," Mom spoke up, which surprised me because I didn't know she'd been paying much attention. She must've been counting the envelopes that came addressed to me. "At one hundred signatures a page, that's more than four thousand."

"Big deal," Kellie said. "So he has four thousand names. If he gets five times that, it's still only going to be twenty thousand."

"It's a real good start, Son," said Dad.

"Right. He'll only be short ... what ... 980,000 signatures." Nicole said.

"Plus he made a complete fool of himself in the process," Kellie added, though it didn't seem like her heart was in the whole insulting-me thing. That's probably because she'd just got a boyfriend and it had put her in a better mood. I figured we might as well enjoy *that* while we could. Once he sees her true colours he'll dump her for sure and she'll be back to being nasty again.

"It's no wonder I never bring my friends here," Nicole said, picking up her usual lament. "You'd think that someone would stop this kind of thing before it even got started, but *no*, that doesn't happen at our house."

"That will do," Mom said, without even glancing up from her food.

"*I* didn't do anything!" Leah protested, as if Mom had spoken directly to her.

"It's a wonder," Kellie said. She rolled her eyes dramatically. "Anyway, it's bad enough we have a quirk for a brother."

"Four thousand is a very respectable start," Dad said.

"Yes it is!" Mom agreed.

I felt good for a few seconds, but then I remembered how they hadn't thought I'd even make it through one weekend without talking. All of a sudden the confidence they were trying to show didn't mean much.

I realized, later on when I got thinking about what Nicole and Kellie had been saying, that I hadn't actually done the math. I mean, I knew I needed a million signatures, but it hadn't occurred to me to stop and see how many pages of signatures I actually needed. So I did that after we'd finished eating.

It was ten thousand! (I realized immediately that Mira *had* figured it out, because the boxes she'd brought were made to hold that exact amount.) Ten thousand pages of names and so far I had forty-three!

I knew in that moment that I'd made a big mistake. I should have gone with something sensible, like Durkin had suggested in the first place.

Then I wondered how much of what I was doing was really for the kids and how much of it was to shut up my guilty conscience for the way the whole thing had started. Maybe there was something to what Bryan had said the day we finished the website.

The really big thing I had to think about, though, was the fact that there was no way I was *ever* going to get a million signatures.

Maybe it's not too late to change the number, I thought. But I knew it was.

I might never be able to talk again.

Chapter Twenty-Five

By the end of the next week I was feeling a bit more encouraged. I'd received another seventy-one petitions by then — and the following week brought in even more, with 111. But the week after that, they started petering out and I only got twenty-six. That brought the entire total up to 251. It was a drop in the bucket.

We were almost at the end of March by then and except for calling myself names the day my voice had come back, I hadn't spoken for almost nine weeks. Maybe I shouldn't even count the first few weeks, when I hadn't exactly been doing it for the right reason, but it had all come together because of that, so I'd let go of the guilt and tried to stay focused on what was really important.

Bryan had an idea around that time that seemed promising. He started contacting head offices of some major companies, to see if they would help the cause by circulating petitions in their stores. Even passing them around among employees would have been a help, and if one of them agreed to post them for customers to see and sign, we figured that would bring in thousands and thousands of pages of signatures.

Only, apparently it wasn't that simple, because no one agreed to do it. It seemed there were legal things to consider. Bryan spent a whole week working on the idea, and in the end it all came to nothing.

He stayed optimistic but I could see he was getting frustrated. He never said so, but I think he was also getting a bit tired of hanging around with someone who didn't talk. I could see how that wouldn't be great, but there was nothing I could do about it.

April came without a lot of hope that I was ever going to see the million mark. I was still getting petitions, but they were just trickling in. Some days there might be four or five, others one or two. A few days there were none. By the middle of the month the total had only grown to 288.

"If it keeps going at this rate," Bryan said one day, "it will take about thirteen years to get the million signatures. Of course, that's assuming the whole thing won't just fall flat at some point."

I shrugged.

"You're not even thinking about giving up yet, are you?" he asked. When I shook my head he stared at me for a minute, shook his too, and then kind of laughed and punched me on the shoulder.

"Then we'd better think of some more ideas," he said, "just in case you happen to come up with something worth saying in the next thirteen years."

It was the next week that things started to happen. One day when I got home from school there was a news van in our driveway. For some reason, I never even connected its presence to what I was doing.

"Griffin!" Mom called out to me as soon as I stepped through the doorway. "There are some people here to see you."

The woman told me her name was Jill and said that she was interested in my story. She also introduced me to a camera guy named Steve and a man named Ivan whose role wasn't clear to me.

"They're from the news!" Mom said, like I was too dumb to realize that on my own. "And not just the local news, either!"

"We're going to help you get your signatures," Jill said then. She tousled my hair, which, instead of annoying me, made me blush.

"Okay, let's do it," she added, turning to the men she'd just introduced. They spun into action, setting things up and picking a spot for filming. I was amazed at how fast they worked. I mean, they'd hardly said hello to me and there they were, ready to film.

They got me to stand beside Jill and she put her free hand on my shoulder. The other hand held her microphone, though it was relaxed at her side until her producer yelled a couple of things. Then she lifted it to her mouth and looked straight ahead.

It was kind of funny how Jill adjusted her face for the filming. One second she was smiling and looking casual and the next instant her expression looked so solemn and concerned you'd think she'd been up all night worrying about this thing.

"I'm here in Westingford at the home of a young man named Griffin Maxwell. Unfortunately, I can't interview Griffin ..."

"No, that's not it." Jill cut herself off, paused for a few seconds and then let them know she was ready to start again.

Her new opening said something about how she was honoured to be my voice, to help me spread a message on behalf of thousands of children worldwide — children who have no one to speak on their behalf. I thought it was pretty good.

After that, she went on and explained about how I hadn't spoken for approximately three months — and why. She explained about the million signatures I was trying to get to help other kids. Then she wrapped it up with a couple of moving sentences and ... the web address for our site!

When they'd finished filming me, they talked about whether or not they should interview some family members. To my huge relief, they decided against it.

"We've got the kid," Jill said, "and a copy of his essay.

If we need to fill a few seconds, we can pan to that and have someone read a line or two. It's not like the network is going to give us a lot of time for this one."

The network didn't. There was nothing extra, and they cut out some of what Jill had filmed with me, but that was no problem. The message came across loud and clear, and that was what mattered.

It aired on the news that night at six and again at ten. Mom taped it, though I don't know why, since all I did was stand there and look basically useless. I'm pretty sure she can see that just about anytime.

I could hardly wait to see Bryan at school the next day, and cornered him in the hallway before classes.

"Why didn't I tell you about the news thing?" he said, reading a note I'd given him. "You're kidding right? I didn't know anything about it until Mira called me up squealing that you were on TV and telling me to turn it on quick. You don't really think I'd have done that without telling you!"

I grabbed the page, scribbled quickly, and passed him the paper again.

"I don't *know* who contacted them. I don't think it was Mira, though. She would have said something. Maybe someone sent them the e-mail we started up."

But I found out that night (at the dinner table — where else?) that it hadn't been an e-mail that had done it.

"How'd you get the news to come here and do a story on you anyway?" Nicole asked.

"He can't talk, 'member?" Leah gave what was her standard reminder by that time, in case anyone had forgotten. In the beginning she'd yell it out and laugh when someone made the mistake, but now she recited it automatically and hardly bothered to look up from her plate.

"Well, I'd sure like to know how he managed to get on the news."

"I think you should tell them, dear," Mom said.

I thought she was talking to me, and looked up to signal her that I really didn't know, either, except I saw that she was looking at Dad. Confused, I turned toward him in time to see him shake his head just slightly.

"*You* did something, Dad?" Nicole asked, catching on before I did.

"Yes, he did!" Mom said. I could see that she'd just barely been holding this information in, and was only too happy to be telling it. "Oh, he didn't want to say anything, but I don't see why. He's too modest sometimes, your father."

Then it came out, thanks to Mom. Apparently, Dad had driven into the city last week and waited for an entire day to see Jill. They kept telling him she was busy, and he just kept saying that was no problem — he'd wait.

Finally, she agreed to give him five minutes. And my dad, the guy who usually stays pretty quiet, somehow managed, in that short of a time, to persuade her that this was important enough for her to do a story about it.

I caught him alone a bit later in the evening, and since I couldn't talk, I passed him a note that just said, "Thanks, Dad!"

"Sure," he said, looking embarrassed. "I hope it helps, Son."

Then, feeling a bit silly about it, I shook his hand. Seemed the thing to do lately.

CHAPTER TWENTY-SIX

I was pretty excited about the news story, so it was disappointing when there was no increase in the petitions that arrived that week. Mom kept telling me to be patient and reminded me that it had only been a few days.

"People have to have time to go to the site, download the form, get the signatures, and send them," she explained to me almost every day that the mail arrived without a big stack of envelopes. "They're not going to be able to get one hundred signatures in a day or two. And even after they've sent the petitions, it takes time for the post office to get them here."

I'd smile and nod to show her I knew that and was okay with it, but if you want the truth, I was losing hope rapidly.

Bryan came by on the weekend to let me know he'd been talking with Mira and she'd told him that the traffic on the website had gone way up.

"You watch," he said, "you'll see results by Monday for sure."

But he was wrong. And when nothing was happening by Tuesday, I knew I had to face the fact that the news story hadn't worked.

I felt bad for my father, since he'd gone to all that trouble and had really believed that this might turn things around.

Since the whole petition thing had started, I'd gotten in the habit of checking to see if there was any mail as soon as I got home from school each day. The next Wednesday was no different and I went straight to the kitchen to see what might have arrived.

My heart sank to see that the table was bare, since Mom puts the mail there everyday. She was sitting at the head of the table, cutting out cookies from rolled dough.

"Hi, dear," she said. She smiled. "Come sit over here and give me a hand with this."

When I was little I used to like to make cookies and stuff with my mom, but I was way too old for that now. Still, she looked so happy at the idea that I couldn't turn her down. I went around the table and pulled out the chair I'd need to sit on to reach the dough and cutters.

Only, there was a bag sitting there already. Then Mom jumped up and grabbed me and hugged me real hard, which was okay since there was no one else around.

"This came for you!" she said, pointing to the bag.

I picked it up, not sure what was going on. When I

opened it, I found that it was jammed full of envelopes! I couldn't move for a minute — I don't know for sure if I was even breathing just then.

"Dump them out," Mom said. "We'll open them and count them together."

I did and we sat down and got busy. Mom quickly suggested that we should make stacks of one hundred and then paperclip them so it would be easier to count the total later on. It took a little while and when we were done we had five stacks of one hundred, plus another thirty-three.

Kellie arrived as we were adding these to the others (which we also divided into piles of a hundred). She looked cross (as usual) scowled at the papers, and demanded to know if Ariel had called. When Mom said she hadn't, Kellie spun around and walked off in a huff, muttering something about friendship being more important than a stupid Science project.

"Ahhh," Mom said.

I looked at her questioningly.

"It seems that your sister is feeling left out because Ariel is spending quite a lot of time working on an assignment — with someone else. I've noticed that she's been a bit ill-tempered lately. That must be why."

Ill-tempered *lately*! At first I thought she must be kidding. I mean, Kellie is never anything *but* ill-tempered!

I might have smirked a bit. I definitely did something to make Mom look at me in a way that told me a lecture was on its way. Her right eyebrow went up and she sighed the way she does when no one except her understands something. It's a sure sign that she's going to try to explain it.

"Now, Griffin. You're old enough to realize that there are reasons your sister — well, not just Kellie of course, but all teenagers — aren't always the most, uh, joyful creatures in the world."

I wished I could take back the smirk that had started this! It was sounding like it might go down one of those roads that mothers like so much. I was right.

Trapped, I stood and pretended to listen while Mom talked about hormones and mood changes and stuff. Thankfully, I was able to block most of it out, but some got through in spite of my best efforts not to hear what she was saying.

I nearly ran out of there (in a perfectly reasonable act of self-defence) when she started saying that very soon changes would be happening *to me too*. What does she think — I'm *seven*? Just because I don't happen to announce things to my mother doesn't mean I'm not well on the road to becoming a man! Talk about insulting.

I must have looked as disgusted as I felt, because her voice trailed off before she had a chance to get into the particulars.

"Well, anyway, I just wanted you to realize that your sister can't always control how she's feeling," she said. It was a lame ending, right back where she'd started, but I was just glad it was over.

I gave her a weak smile and nod, grabbed the box of petitions, and took off down the hall. Once I was inside my room I even locked the door, just in case.

To distract myself from the narrow escape, I did some calculating to see how long it would take to get the million signatures if I got a bagful of petitions like today's every day. After playing around with the numbers a bit, I figured three or four weeks should do it, supposing I got five hundred a day for the next while.

I was pretty happy about that, and was actually starting to look forward to being able to talk again. I decided another month wouldn't be any problem at all.

But, it didn't turn out quite like that.

Thursday and Friday the bags of letters were bigger and heavier. Monday, there were three bags. Tuesday, eight! I couldn't believe my eyes and Mom was starting to look a bit frazzled with her kitchen being taken over by mail.

Dad suggested that we move the operation (as he called it) into the living room and all of a sudden everyone was pitching in. That sure helped, because opening all of those envelopes and counting them took a lot more time than you'd expect.

The girls actually pitched in without complaining, and I noticed that they weren't quite as nasty to me as usual. I think it was affecting them, that all these people had cared enough to help, and they couldn't help getting caught up in the spirit of the whole thing.

Bryan came along and helped as much as he could, especially on the weekends. Mira brought more boxes when I told her we were running out. The four boxes she'd brought would have been enough to hold that many sheets of new paper, but the petitions had been folded, and even flattened back out they took up more space.

"You need any more help?" she asked. Her voice was hopeful.

I motioned her in and was glad when Nicole told her emphatically that we needed every bit of help we could get.

I even found that I didn't really mind having her there. She's not as bad as I used to think.

You're probably jumping to conclusions about that, aren't you? Assuming that things turned around and I started liking her or whatever? Well, that didn't happen.

What did happen was a bit of a surprise to me, because Mira paused at the door one night when she was leaving and broke it to me.

"Look, Griffin, I still like you, but, uh, just as a friend. So, I'm breaking our date for the dance, okay?"

Okay? I nodded, in a kind of stunned way because it was a bit of a shock. But I'm pretty sure I was happy about it.

It wasn't until the next day that I found out what had changed her mind.

"So, dude, you're okay with the Mira thing?" Bryan

asked. He didn't look at me. Then it came out! Mira was going to the dance with *him* instead. Seems they'd been talking a lot and stuff and decided they liked each other. Talk about a twist!

Anyway, the main thing was that I was off the hook.

Two weeks after the first bag of mail had arrived we were sorting and stacking as usual when Kellie jumped up and went for a calculator. She punched in some figures and then let out a little shriek.

"You have almost eleven thousand petitions! That's more than a million signatures! You can talk again!" She jumped up and down a few times and actually hugged me before she realized what she was doing.

"Not bad for a doofus," she added. But then she laughed and hugged me again.

"Hey! He could have talked yesterday," Bryan said. And he was right. It was actually kind of cool to think that we'd been so wrapped up in what we were doing that we'd lost sight of that part of it.

But now — I could talk again. I felt a big smile spreading across my face.

"So, c'mon, Griff, say something!" Nicole said.

"Yeah!" they all chorused. Then Bryan stood up and started clapping, and so did Mira, and then everyone joined in.

"Speech!" they demanded.

Which, I'm sure you remember, is how this whole thing started.

Epilogue

Griffin John Maxwell maintained his protest of silence for a total of 114 days. Even after he began to speak again, petitions continued to pour in as thousands and thousands of people joined him in supporting the cause that had become so important to him.

In all, more than three million signatures were gathered and forwarded to government officials.

The following year, Griffin Maxwell gave a speech.

As he stood nervously looking out at a circle of faces, he wondered how he could do it. Those familiar feelings were back: pounding heart, sweaty palms, and dry mouth.

Griffin paused and looked down at the page in his hand. Then he drew a deep breath, cleared his throat and began to speak.

"At this time last year, I was silent. It was an experience I can never regret, because of what it taught me. Perhaps the greatest thing I learned was that it is not silence that is powerful — it is action and speech.

"The fight against children being used in armed conflict is far from over and I firmly believe that the best thing we can do is unite our voices and speak out — speak out as loud and as long as it takes — until all children, everywhere, are safe."

As he finished his speech, thunderous applause broke out and Griffin's audience rose to its feet, smiling with pride and approval.

The standing ovation Griffin received that day did not come from his classmates. Rather, it came from the Members of Parliament, which Griffin had been invited to address because of his remarkable efforts on behalf of child soldiers.

But Griffin barely saw his audience. His focus was on the page that he held firmly in his hand, and the face that smiled back at him from that page.

The face of Kato Musamba, child of war.

Kato Musamba escaped from the Lord's Resistance Army after almost four years in captivity. Although he is once again in Uganda, it has not been safe for him to return to his village. He has seen his parents and his sister, Nagesa, once since his escape.

Kato's brother Paskar and his other sister Sudati were captured by the LRA along with Kato. Paskar was murdered because his feet had become cracked and swollen and he was unable to keep up with the others.

Sudati's whereabouts are unknown at this time.

Kato struggles daily to overcome the horrors of life in the LRA. Although he made an attempt to resume his schooling he was unable to focus on his studies.

Today, Kato works as a field hand in a southern Ugandan village.

God Bless the Child.

Suggested Resource Information on Child Soldiers:

Internet
Amnesty International:
Australia: www.amnesty.org.au
Canada: www.amnesty.ca
U.S.A.: www.amnestyusa.org
United Kingdom: www.amnesty.org.uk
Human Rights Watch: www.hrw.org
Coalition to Stop the Use of Child Soldiers:
www.child-soldiers.org
Government of Canada:
www.waraffectedchildren.gc.ca/menu-en.asp

Major Child Sponsorship Organizations
Foster Parents Plan International Inc:
Canada: Foster Parents Plan of Canada:
www.FosterParentsPlan.ca
U.S.A.: www.planus.org
World Vision:
Canada: www.worldvision.ca
United Kingdom: www.worldvision.org.uk
U.S.A.: www.worldvision.org
Child Fund International:
Canada: www.canadianchristianchildrensfund.ca
U.S.A.: christianchildrensfund.org

Acknowledgements

As always, I am grateful to those whose continuing support and encouragement have made my dream a reality.

My husband, partner, and best friend, Brent. Until the sky falls down on me.

My parents, Bob and Pauline Russell.

My son Anthony, his lovely wife Maria, and daughters Emilee and Ericka. My daughter Pamela and her husband, David Jardine. My brothers and their families: Danny and Gail; Andrew, Shelley and Bryce. My "other" family: Ron and Phoebe Sherrard, Ron Sherrard and Dr. Kiran Pure, Bruce and Roxanne Mullin, and Karen Sherrard.

Special thanks to Allan Carter, whose invitation to me to judge speeches at a local school gave birth to the idea that eventually formed this story.

Friends: Janet Aube, Jimmy Allain, Karen Arseneault, Karen Donovan, Angi Garofolo, John Hambrook, Sandra Henderson, Jim Hennessy, Alf Lower, Mary Matchett, Johnnye Montgomery, Marsha Skrypuch, Linda Stevens, Ashley Smith, Pam Sturgeon, Paul Theriault, and Bonnie Thompson.

At The Dundurn Group, the whole team and particularly my awesome editor, Barry Jowett, whose thoughtful direction added strength to this story.

Readers! Hearing from you is the best part of writing, and I love getting your letters and e-mails. Special thanks to Haley Baker, Conor Bradshaw, Conor Bryant, Bryanna Buchanan, Alaura Campbell, Cat Filippov, Pete Lafrance, Kelly Giovenazzo, Margaret Girodat, Lindsay Hansen, Sammy MacDonald, Kailey Metcalfe, Alisa Murray, Calla Pfrimmer, Katherine Reid, John Teau, and Jordyn Wade.

You are on these pages and they belong to you.